The Witch and The Lich

D. E. Stone

Published by Motley Mince LC, 2022.

Table of Contents

Dedication

This book has three dedications First, to my grandfather, who walked in on me pacing in his basement telling myself stories and asked what I was doing. Without his suggestion that I should write all of this down, I probably never would have thought to write any of this down. Equally, to my wife, who spent a month enthusiastically reading my roughest drafts and decided that she needed to share them with everyone who would listen. Without all of her hard work, this book wouldn't be in your hands today.

Of no lesser importance is my final dedication. This book is dedicated to you, reader. Without you, I'm just a man with a head full of ideas, pacing in the dark. Thank you for bringing my words into your life and letting them grow into a story. I hope its one you'll like.

We also want to thank all the wonderful people who contributed to the crowdfunding campaign to publish this book:

Kaitlyn Rose Meyers
Mark Baldwin
Danniale Casey
Adam Palmer
Rebecca Smeltzer
Kayla McGuire
Renee Ally
Erika Aragona
Brenda Ellis
Adam Palmer
Jonah Smith
Petra Briar
Melissa Murone
Ryane Logsdon
Elizabeth Zubritsky
Alexa Thompson
Jayce McKinney, Thank you all!

Chapter 1
In Which Protocol Is Not Followed, To Mixed Results

Krell Casat had now been dead longer than he had been alive. It was his 192nd death-day, and he was no happier now than the day he died to still be around. After 175 years of service to the Imperial Navy, a personal relationship to the late Emperor, and enough blood on his hands to drown a battalion, he felt that the least he was owed was a visit from Death Herself, one now long overdue.

"We have you surrounded! Surrender at once!" called an officer from beyond the makeshift barricade. Krell glanced in the side mirror of the overturned transport he'd taken cover behind. He could make out two artillery pieces and at least as many platoons of troopers. They'd deployed several mobile cover units and had their weapons trained on what remained of the caravan Krell had bartered with for passage. The caravan guards had put up as much of a fight as could be expected under the circumstances, but four of them were already down and the rest had dashed into the treeline, leaving him alone and in the line of fire.

That creeping voice that had been adhered to him when the necromantic enchantments had turned him into this, skeletal thing, was trying to worm its way into his reserves of magic. Krell knew that even without the destructive power of a lich, this did not constitute a severe challenge to a man of his skills. He touched a hand to his rib cage, holding an image of the locket within in his mind's eye, and quietly centered himself. He never missed having lungs as much as he did when he needed to calm down.

"First squad, advance on that vehicle. Fourth platoon, get up on the ridge and try to flank him. He's still in there, I'm sure of it."

Fourth platoon, now that did a lot to clarify the situation. Standard unit organization hadn't changed since the last Hierarch had been deposed, which meant that he was probably up against a field artillery company. There would be six platoons of infantry, two artillerist platoons with their respective cannons, a logistical platoon to drive everyone around, and a platoon of field engineers to keep all the vehicles running and tell everyone where not to dig if they needed a trench. Protocol absolutely never would have allowed such a unit to be deployed against a merchant caravan.

Putting aside his critique of the tactical decisions being made by the opposition commander, Krell was in the unfortunate position of knowing exactly how to handle the situation, and knowing how happy it was going to make the lich to do it. He pulled himself upright, drifting into the air involuntarily.

"I wish to speak with your commanding officer." The troopers held their fire as they watched the robed, skeletal figure suspended in midair above the damaged vehicles. He felt their heartbeats begin to quicken as several of them recognized his form and they realized their own odds of survival in a fight. Liches weren't common enough to be met in every trooper's career, but they were common enough to make an appearance in the training material. The fear flowed from them into their surroundings, and from there it began trickling into his magical reserves. The lich swelled in him with the growing power.

"Krell Casat, I am Major Ulnor Harthgow of Decidua. You are under arrest by order of Empress Holine the Fourth. Stand down and comply or we will be forced to bring you in by force."

Of course she did. Holine had never let him rest before, why would she let him go now?

"Good Morning Major Harthgow. I have a message for her Imperial Majesty." The officer blinked. He must be new at this. "I swore by my breath and blood to serve the Empire. I no longer breathe, and I cannot be made to bleed, so I don't think it's unreasonable to believe I also no longer can be made to serve." He could see the man choking on his own tongue. "If she wants anything from me, she can have it over my dead body." One of the troopers tilted back, his gun lowering. It was nice to see that the rank and file still had a sense of humor.

"What are you laughing at?" The trooper straightened, "He's chosen force, apply it!"

Before they could act on the order, Krell raised his left hand, thumb extended upward, and sighted out the artillery piece up the road, just a kilometer off. Then, a gravelly whisper joined the faint clatter of his skeletal hand clenching at the distant weapon, stone and earth burst from beneath the offending object and buried it halfway into the earth. He felt the pain of its crew surging through him, giving him strength well beyond that which he had expended on his spells. The lich's joy was a mirror of the death grin Krell could not escape. Just a little more destruction and they would have the power to destroy Holine and be free.

Krell pushed that thought back down. He didn't want to destroy Kevand's daughter, only to be free of her control. Even if he did, he would never allow himself to do so at the expense of an innocent life. He brushed the air lightly, cracking open the emergency hatches on the two artillery pieces, allowing the crew inside, although injured, to escape.

"Please, Major, if you insist on fighting, draw your weapon and face me alone. We can settle this like men, or we can settle this like monsters," Krell called out to the officer, hoping that he would see reason before the increasing rush of power allowed the lich to overtake him.

The officer shouted to his men to keep firing. None of them obeyed. They all knew it wouldn't help. Imperial anti-mage drills included a very clear lesson about knowing your threat level. Official policy was that anyone who can dispatch your supporting artillery with one hand was someone you should keep a safe distance from and allow your superior officer to handle. Apparently, this officer did not care to do his part.

"I'll have all of you court martialed for this! Someone shoot him!" he shouted, a mixture of fear and anger in his voice. He knew he was out of his league, he should have notified his commander. Krell had actually planned on using the withdrawal as an opportunity to escape. Now, with the Major insisting on endangering his men in a wasteful engagement, that was no longer an option. If one of his officers had acted with such blatant disrespect for the lives of their men, they would have been put in front of a tribunal and likely thrown in the brig.

One of the troopers began to draw his sword to charge, but Krell drew a bead on him with one hand and the man let go of the hilt and stepped away. His commander drew his sidearm and matched Krell's aim.

"Cowards! I'll teach you to disobey orders."

The Lich could never have dreamed of matching Krell's reaction time in that moment. Ten meters was a drop in the bucket from the reserves of power Krell now had access to. Their was a pop as space distorted to allow him to move without crossing the distance, and even without muscles the ferocity of Krell's grasp was enough to push the weapon aloft and send his shot wide. He drew upon the heartless man's own surprise, and turned it into a wave of flame that rushed over him with a brief orange light. The lich laughed as the last of the man's life force was pulled into them. Krell strained as the darkness rose up within him, and thought of the destination his companions had spoken of, a warehouse in Theapastaly. He pushed all the magic he could into the spell, and vanished.

• • • •

Krell found himself in a crowded room. He pushed one of the nearby crates aside as gently as he could in his weakened state. Crowded, he thought, was the wrong word. Cluttered would be a better description.

Crowded implied a crowd, cluttered implied an excess of disorganized objects. A room full of haphazardly stacked crates, loose tablets, and what he suspected was some sort of food wrappers, was very definitely cluttered.

He pulled himself upright, trying not to place too much weight on any single item. The teleportation had drained him, even with the power he'd just gained by murdering the hapless, if uncouth officer. He could stand, but there would need to be some measure of suffering and fear before he could do any more serious spell casting. A public sighting, or cornering a local thief should suffice to prepare him for the next encounter, unfortunate as that would be.

A crashing sound echoed from not too far away. Krell ducked into cover as he began scanning his surroundings. The room looked to be some manner of storeroom, about 6 meters tall and no more than 15 meters long. The crates were of consistent size and unmarked. He grabbed one of the tablets, turned it on, and dimmed the screen quickly. Within a few moments, he was able to determine that it contained a number of shipping manifests, mostly toys and small entertainment items. It didn't make sense to him. The crates seemed too plain for entertainment, but he didn't have time to check before a beam of light began to scan the room.

Krell didn't need to question the nature of the light. The under-barrel lamp of a standard Imperial Blaster was quite familiar to him. Krell began to consider his options as the light passed by him.

"Nothing out of place in this one sir. I think it was just the local vermin," The soldier shouted over his shoulder toward the room he had entered from.

"Probably. Come on back," replied a voice from out of sight. "Don't know what we did to get stuck with the old coot. Surely there's a nice princess somewhere, looking for a chance to prove her worth, we could be serving under, am I right?"

"Don't be crass Jerry. Besides, he can probably hear you," The trooper turned and began to walk out. Krell quietly slid himself around to keep an eye on this departing man. He waited quietly until the man had been out for several seconds, and could be trusted not to return. At last, he popped back out of cover and began to cautiously edge toward the door. He found a stack of crates by the door and crouched as low as possible. There were more voices down the hall, and a fair few of them sounded afraid. Krell felt his feet lift from the ground as the muffled shouts and atmosphere of terror wafted up the hall. Even this little amount of power was such an improvement over his prior weakness, like water to a man in the desert. He moved toward the entrance to the hall, the voices growing more clear as he drifted.

"Indeed. I suspect that attitude is precisely why you're assigned this detail, Jerrold. They tend to send the best to the locations likely to lend themselves to a more dramatic showdown," The voice had the distinctive twinge of a voice modulator. It could have meant any number of things, but Krell suspected it was an Imperial Guard. He checked the tablet for Optics, and quickly angled it around the corner to confirm his fears.

The warehouse itself was large, though the ceiling was not high. The room Krell peered out of was one of eight that branched off of a central hub, which was mostly open. In the center of the room was a tall figure in ornate armor seated at a receptionist's desk, and near each wing stood two troopers, much like the ones he had just left by the roadside. There were six other men, dressed in more common clothes, stained with sweat and reeking of fear. There were two troopers nearby with their weapons trained on this small crew of what Krell could only imagine were the smugglers operating out of this warehouse. But none of the people within merited so much attention as the one seated behind the small desk.

The Imperial Guard had a very stable uniform throughout the ages. The distinctive half-cape hanging from the left pauldron, reinforced heavy armor that shimmered with enchantments, and blood red staff would have been identifiable to a child of 6. Krell's concern deepened as he began to recognize the details of the uniform; small notches in the uncloaked pauldron identified him as a Lieutenant and patches sewn into the blue green cape were reminders of battles fought. This Guard belonged to company 13; an elite unit made up entirely of officers and bodyguards retired from prior appointments. Holine had flushed him out with a patsy and he'd walked into one of her most experienced warriors.

Krell stowed the tablet into his robes. It had been a long time since he'd been to the palace, but this might work to his advantage. If not, well, it wasn't as though he were running out of time.

"Now, if none of you have seen the rebel, I'm afraid we will have to settle in until we receive further instructions." Several feet shuffled uncomfortably. "I imagine there's at least one deck of cards in all this, why don't we play a round of dominion while we wait? I'm sure that word will be out within an hour." Someone must have had a pack near at hand, because the momentary quiet was broken by the sound of shuffling. Krell let the old guard play the first few rounds before enacting his plan. As the fear began to subside in the room beyond, the Lich turned the ring on his finger, and slipped silently into the hall.

What the ring held was not a simple enchantment. It had been a gift from a passerby who did not seem to understand the value of what he held. Nonetheless, it was indeed valuable. True invisibility was no complex thing, but many defenses existed against it. Wards could be cast against its effects and many forms of technology did not rely on the visible spectrum. What Krell used now, was a perception filter, far harder to combat. He passed a pair of troopers, both ignoring him without so much as a glance. A third, Jerold apparently, mimed shooting himself as Krell approached the veteran guardsman. Krell sat down, drawing himself a hand as he did so.

"Good of you to join us," the Guard set down three of his cards. Krell glanced at his own hand, selected a handful and replied in kind. It was a terrible hand, and the guard took the round easily when they revealed their cards.

"It is the responsibility of all citizens to show the Guard respect and not obstruct them in performance of their duties. I am merely doing my part." Krell drew replacement cards, finding them no better than his opening hand.

"Still, it's nice to not make a scene once in a while." Both played their cards, evenly matched this time. Krell reached for the deck, only to have his hand stopped by the guard. "It hasn't been the same since you left, Admiral."

Krell could not smile, though a pale grin was unavoidable in his current state.

"Not many still live who knew me as such. Who do I owe the pleasure?"

"Olan. You avenged my father at Cariol. We've never had a chance to meet in person."

"Now that was a long time ago." Krell could remember the rime-clad knight standing over the fallen guard. As he reflected, he felt the whispering dark promise that he could be like the accursed warrior, strong and unstoppable. Krell shook it off, the Frostbourne warlord held no power he craved. "I'm sorry about your father. He was a good man, and his service should never be forgotten." The guard released his hand, drawing his own cards in preparation for the next round.

"I had come prepared to repay the debt with my own life." He glanced around at the oblivious troopers. "It would seem that will not be necessary."

"I hope so." Krell played his best hand of the game, losing once again by an easy three points. "Perhaps you could help me find passage off world?"

Before Olan could reply, a trooper entered from a side door. "Sir, we have new orders. Guardsman Tren's squad didn't report in and we're being ordered to meet up with Mag and Kulo's squads and investigate."

His shoulders raised and straightened "Let them know we're on our way." He glanced back at Krell. "Tren is across the street from Gasca's finest pastry shop. I'm sure he's lost track of time while glutting himself on their infamous tarts. I look forward to trying them myself shortly after we arrive." He set down his cards, another winning hand clearly on display. "I doubt there's anything I could do to help you escape. Off world teleportation is being diverted. The 19th fleet is parked in orbit on full patrol. Any unidentified ships will be disabled and boarded. If you can lay low, I'd advise it. If you're lucky, that ring might get you unnoticed onto a ship, but you'd need the right documentation to get past the checkpoint."

"Any suggestions on how to obtain such documentation?"

"Sorry, I'm afraid not. Good luck." Olan tapped his staff and motioned the troopers to the door, a faint glow fading from his staff. Krell suspected it was a glamour to hide their conversation. It was unnecessary with the ring, but he appreciated the precaution.

One of the smugglers blurted out a single laugh. "Even we couldn't get you the paperwork to sneak onto a ship right now. You might as well ask The Witch for favors." One of his companions smacked him lightly, gesturing an apology to the Guard.

"The who?" Krell had nearly forgotten the warehouse's owners, still sitting in the corner, terrified of the soldiers.

"You've never heard of the Witch?"

"Of course he ain't heard of the Witch! Fine folk like them don't mess around with the depths of the Net with grime-fingered louts like you."

"I'm terribly sorry. Perhaps just a simple explanation?" Krell felt a quiet, icy voice crawling into his mind, reminding him that he could probably kill Olan and his troops all at once if he struck now. He ground his teeth and ignored the voice. "I've never had more than a casual interaction with the Net."

The older of the two smugglers gave his partner a smug glance. "The Witch is a legend among us Net divers. Every time you see that someone anonymously tipped off the authorities to a pedophile, or leaked the details of a shady business deal, it was the Witch. She's some kind of an Alpha level admin for the whole Net, no one can see what she does, or even prove she exists. Like an Angel in the System."

"Or a Demon. Don't you forget the rumors she's behind all those disappearances."

"Disappearances?" Krell asked. The doors closed behind Olan and his troopers as they left the warehouse.

"Yeah, but they were all bigwigs and fancy folk. Immortals hiding in the open."

"Sure, the ones we know about. What's to say she doesn't kill normal folk when she gets the itch?"

Krell held up a hand. "This Witch might be able to help me get off world without being caught?"

Both smugglers thumbed an affirmative. "How might I contact her?" The younger smuggler shrugged. The older replied, "same way you get ahold of any admin, probly. No one's ever done it on purpose before that I've heard of."

Krell drew the tablet from his robes, opened the Net and clicked the help button. A conversation opened and he began to type.

Chapter Two

In Which A Lich Contacts Tech Support

ontact Net Admin: The Witch

C Krell got an error message saying that no admin under that identity existed. There was always the help function's search bar. It seemed like a terrible place to start, but where else were you supposed to get in touch with a Net Admin? For all his other experience, the Net had always escaped his understanding.

"No spaces in usernames, use an underscore." Commented one of the smugglers as they began repacking the various crates the troopers had overturned in their search.

"And never capitalize articles, dincha take any computing classes?" snarked another.

"It's been a long time. But thank you." He decided not to risk his luck on working in a room where apparently everyone was reading over his shoulder. He typed into the search function again.

Contact Net Admin: the_Witch

As he wafted toward the door, a little less confident in his disguise, he stared blankly at the helpful suggestions of 'meet talented witches in your area' and 'Chirugeons hate her, find out how Olianora lost 40 pounds in five minutes and you can too!'. It wasn't as though Witches weren't talented or powerful, though he had met few himself, it was simply that the Net was a terrible place for unrefined research.

Krell glanced about. No ambush awaited him; Olan was true to his word. He drifted out into the morning light of the alley, and made his way toward the street. He refined his query.

Contact Net Admin: the_Witch

The tablet returned a lost signal page. He drifted back into the warehouse and refreshed the search. A quick glance at the two men inside revealed that they were having the same problem. Not a technical problem then, or at least not one with the tablet. He'd have to find somewhere with a more reliable connection. Not that it would be difficult, it was probably just the local authorities blocking the signal to prevent anyone from spreading word of the ongoing search. He just needed to find somewhere densely populated where an outage wouldn't be permissible. He turned and continued toward the street.

Gasca was a pretty big planet. Not physically, it was about the same size as most inhabitable worlds, and its population was actually below the Imperial Average, but it was surprisingly busy for its population density though. People in clothes of every imaginable color shared the streets of the city with a handful of pack animals and a few trams. The cobblestone streets were clean, and the local watch seemed comfortably dressed. Down at the end of the block, across the corner, there was a shop with a sign advertising Fairn's Finery featuring a cheerful looking overweight man admiring a sun bonnet, presumably Fairn. Krell pulled up his hood to hide his bare skull from Fairn's impressively fleshy face, then began toward what appeared to be a local park.

The park wasn't being used in any formalized way at the moment, just a few locals out for a stroll, a gaggle of adolescents loitering on and about a large rock under a few trees, and a man teaching his daughter to fly a kite, and failing quite well. Krell watched the kite flying pair for a while, transfixed and lost in memory. After what felt like only a few moments, the pair crashed the kite badly enough that it could no longer be attempted again. The two began to walk away from the slowly setting sun, and Krell looked back down to the tablet.

Contact Admin: the_Witch

Signal lost. Krell stared at it for a moment. The signal resumed. He searched again

Local area signal strength; History

No signal interruptions since the previous week, and then only for a few moments because of a bit of errant solar activity. Something was fishy about this.

Contact Admin: the_Witch

Signal lost. Krell felt an urge to replace the machine. The signal resumed after, and he counted the seconds, precisely ten minutes. He queried again, timed it, and saw the exact same result. This was a deliberate outage.

Admin Contact Protocol?

-Type 'Contact Admin: [any/specific]. Be Polite, we're very busy and will do our best to help.

Do Admins have the authority to cause a Net outage?

-Admins may suspend access to their Net region if deemed necessary, with approval from senior Admins.

Who is the local Senior Admin?

-Access to that information is restricted for staff safety. Users must have a Class V or higher clearance to access Net Admin identities.

Now there was a problem he could solve. If he was prepared for the risk. The last rays of sunlight were still peeking over the nearby buildings, and many shops had closed. There was a small Restaurant at the far corner of the park, and he could hear the sound of music coming from its second-floor windows. It was far enough away that no one could see him, and with his perception filter, it seemed unlikely that anyone would be able to read over his shoulder. Krell swiftly hovered across the even, well-kept grass of the park into the vicinity of Alpha's Steakhouse, a Gascan chain specializing in Ga-Vok cuisine. They'd run their music off of a shared playlist over the Net. If there was an outage now, it would be instantly recognized. And if they traced his login, there'd be a crowd to disappear into.

Krell opened the User Login, signed out whomever's profile he'd been using with a momentary regret for whoever he'd probably gotten put on a watch list, and then began to enter his own login for the first time in over a hundred years. His old Class II clearance would get him access to just about everything not restricted to the Imperial family and the Guard.

Contact Admin: the_Witch

Krell stared as the tablet froze. His query stayed in the corner, and the signal stayed up. It felt like days passed while he waited for a response. He was sure that she was real, now he just had to wait for her response. Finally, the Tablet opened a new page entirely.

-I thought you were dead. This is going to be so much easier.

• • • •

Rea had never been much for mornings. Luckily, nothing about her work was impeded by wasting sunlight. She rolled out of bed, picked up her tablet and saw the usual array of notifications. A tablet in Gasca wanted to speak with the_Witch, the Technology Support Admin on Tara was providing notification of the weekly server maintenance, and she had the usual unfathomable amount of ads. She sat down at her terminal and initiated a program to divert relevant ads to the tablet on Gasca, and cleared the weekly reset. She ran her probe for the usual threats; news of unexpected supernatural events, sightings of immortals, and anything out of the usual. Then she got dressed for the day.

Her dye job was holding up fine, and none of her shoes needed replacement. She pulled on her gloves, wrapped her arms, pulled on her steelsilk armor, and then wrapped her face. More than a few talismans were stowed throughout the wrappings, along with her tablet, no point in taking risks after all. You never knew what might happen on the way to coffee.

Her tablet buzzed. That tablet in Gasca was asking to speak with her directly. She pulled up the local grid, hard rebooted it, and pulled up security footage of Cafe Sidhe. They were well past the morning rush, but not quite at lunch. She twisted the base of her door knob, checking the plethora of wards and locks affixed to her apartment.

"Cafe Sidhe, you know the one, if you'd please?" she asked. The door swung open to the fragrant smell of coffee, cream, and fresh pastry. "Thank you, I'll be back shortly." Then she stepped through the door, and into the cafe, tapping her tablet to scramble the security camera as she did.

The patrons looked up with a start at the unusual girl. She walked casually to the counter, set her tablet on the counter, drew her wallet and counted out change.

"House blend, small but put it in a large cup."

The middle-aged woman behind the counter looked at her with a small amount of confusion, but prepared the coffee, took the change, and handed over her receipt with a nod. Rea took her drink over to the coffee cart, and brought the cup from black to light tan, then added several heaping spoonfuls of sugar. She drank it for the sake of habit, not the taste. After all, habits made the years pass by faster. She took her coffee, walked over to the nearest door, and quietly said, "I'm ready to go now."

The door opened to her apartment, smelling faintly of dust and old coffee, and she walked through. The door closed behind her as she set down her coffee on the counter in the dusty kitchenette before restoring the security footage in Cafe Sidhe. There was a knock at the door and Rea groaned.

"Show me."

As she spoke, the door became transparent, revealing the familiar form of an old friend, a woman a little older than herself with platinum hair and an icy elemental that wound throughout the hall both beginning and ending at her feet, each of them carrying a few sacks of groceries. Rea motioned for the door to open, then picked up her coffee and walked to the corner of her small apartment that served as a dining area. The woman followed behind her, setting the bags on the counter.

"Good morning Rea. Anything good in your reports today?" The elemental sat not so much beside his companion, as all around her, his vast mane flowing outward from a small otter-like head. The woman reclined into the mists of her familiar, resting one hand on otter's back, and tracing sigils in the air with the other before drawing a frosted glass from beyond sight.

Rea smiled, then pulled up her tablet. "Seclora and the Nielda continue to wage shadow war in the border regions. Petra has been hard at work, as usual."

"It would be news if she were not." Rea chuckled, then continued reading.

"The body of a mage was found not far from Eldriel, autopsy shows cause of death as fear-induced heart attack. Seems like your brother's work. Someone should check in on him."

"If that homebody has killed this mage, then I have no doubt it was a reasoned course of action, but I'll speak with him if he'll allow it," the woman replied before sipping some frothy, steaming drink from her icy glass. "Anything else?"

Rea's eyes narrowed. The last one wasn't terribly unprecedented, but something seemed off about it.

"Empress Holine the Fourth has dispatched the Guard and mobilized the local garrison forces on Gasca to hunt down a Lich."

"That seems excessive. A squad of Guardsman should be more than adequate to deal with a Lich. What is it about this particular Lich that has her dander up?"

Rea barely heard her. She was double checking the search protocol to see why the story had shown up at all. She took another sip of her coffee flavored cream and glanced through the whole story. A bit of propagandizing, something about the Empress' agents tracking this Lich entering the country from the border regions, suspected history with the Secloran military, sowing terror in vulnerable parts of their nation in order to stir up aggression against the Nielda. Rea already knew that Holine's own agents had been responsible for many of the acts attributed to this Lich, and she had the documentation to prove it if she ever cared to. But something wasn't quite lining up.

"She's blaming him for a lot of the nonsense she's been stirring up between them and the Seclorans. It's all stuff her own agents did. Not sure why she'd deflect the blame for things no one even suspects her of though."

"My mother would have called it 'controlling the narrative.'" The otter snorted derisively. Thalia, the Dark Lady of Gravaga, wasn't well loved in most circles, although respected in most for her thousand years of carefully planned and narratively satisfying terror. "Still," she continued, "I think it'd be more likely that she is trying to eliminate a rogue agent."

"But where would Holine have gotten a Lich willing to work for her? They're not exactly known for advertising their skills."

The room darkened a little. Rea focused on her friend as the otter retreated to his mistress. His head rested on her knee as he put a paw in her hand and looked up with kindly, round eyes.

"It is far easier to make a Lich than it is to recruit one, Rea. It takes a great force of will, and a strong desire for power to rule. How much more would it take to command a Lich?" The light slowly began to return to the room as the small white otter began to roll about in the air, riding some unseen slide around Rea's guest.

"I'm sorry Kate, I never really thought about where they all came from. I didn't mean to remind you of...it."

"I despise bloodshed Rea. I always have. You know this." She sighed and traced her fingers across the otter's spine as it elongated, twisting through the air. "Are you certain you will not act against Holine, end this war before it begins?"

Rea rolled her eyes, "I don't do that, Kate. I'm not Tala, intervening wherever I please. And I'm not your mother, guiding the fates of nations. I just keep the sanctity of mortality against those forces that seek to corrupt it." Kate gave her a resigned stare.

"Very well I suppose. Don't hesitate to contact me if things change." She stood, the snow dissipating into the air as she rose. "Whenever you're ready Zee."

With that, Kate lifted her hand daintily. The spectral otter shrank, bounding under her dress before she stepped beyond sight with a quiet pop.

· · · ·

After continuing about her business for much of the day, inspecting a variety of security footage, confidential government documents, and manipulating minutiae for a half dozen ongoing projects, few of them her own, Rea was finally ready to start her evening workout before popping out for dinner. The work was tiresome, but it helped the endless years pass. Her tablet buzzed halfway through her thirteenth crunch. She glanced over and saw, for the second time that day, that a tablet on Gasca was attempting to contact her directly. She killed its local connection, and was halfway through her workout before it buzzed again. She killed it a third time and finished her workout.

That was when an alarm went off. Someone was attempting to query the database for admin identities. It wasn't one of her more serious alarms, just a single high, shrill note. She sat back down at her terminal, pulled up the alarm and began inspecting the user profile. It was a minor Gascan Criminal, smuggling apparently. There was nothing too serious in his profile, barely warranted attention from the authorities. He mostly just transported fenced goods. However, he had attempted to contact her four times in the past 24 hours, and that was far more concerning. Once would have been annoying, but it hadn't even occurred to her that it could be the same person. Usually officials would talk to each other before trying to find her, and most would give up as long as no problem arose. She traced his location in the security grid and cross referenced it with his criminal records.

Nothing.

Or rather, he and his tablet did not seem to line up. He was at home with his parents, eating dinner. It looked pretty good too, although that may have been her appetite thinking for her. His tablet was in a central park elsewhere in the city, near a popular chain restaurant. What was unusual was that she didn't see it. There wasn't anyone suspicious in the park: a late night jogger listening to music, a couple kissing on an isolated bench, and a pale figure in a monk's habit typing on his tablet from a bench facing the busy eatery.

Rea nearly fell out of her chair when the next alarm sounded. A blaring "whoop", someone had used the profile of a high-clearance official from a previously registered device. She hit a dramatically large blue button labeled 'Prioritize Access' before it could flag Imperial monitoring programs. Whatever asshole wanted her attention, he had it, and no one was going to get in her way. A message popped up on screen.

-High Admiral Krell Casat (Deceased) would like to initiate a direct connection

She glanced at the security feed and saw that the Monk had stopped typing, the jogger had moved out of the park, and the couple were decidedly unlikely to deliberately message anyone. She pulled up the Admiral's profile, hoping to get a better feel for his abilities. Dead 194 years, close friend to the late Emperor, unremarkable private life, well beloved by both his men and the public, died suddenly and younger than usual for a mage of his caliber without signs of struggle. The man looked so damn nice on paper she had to double check her own records to make sure he wasn't a practicing diabolist. Then, she started checking for references to his death in the Class I Clearance files.

There were grave records, and post funeral documentation, all signed by Holine herself. This wasn't unusual for a man of his rank. What was unusual was that she had also signed off on an exhumation authorization and denial of exhumation rights. You could say what you wanted about the Bureau of Records and History, but they were very thorough. She checked the time of Exhumation against the security footage and saw the Empress herself, with a pair of Guards, standing over the grave. There was a flash of light, the Guards decapitated both diggers with sudden blows, and both bodies were rolled into the grave as Holine helped a skeletal figure from it. Rea paused the feed and slid back from her desk.

Kate was right. Holine had made a Lich. A quick perusal of the next hundred and fifty years of Imperial Prerogative Action Summaries showed activity under an operation named 'Uncle' that lined up obscenely well with the rap sheet Holine had attributed to the mystery Lich her Guards had been hunting that very morning on Gasca. Krell Casat had been turned into an unliving weapon. In all her years, Rea could honestly say that she had seen far, far worse, but this sort of thing rubbed her the wrong way.

Rea stepped away, and went to check her book. It was, as always, in a side holster hanging on her steelsilk shirt. She lifted the book, the life's work of her late father, opened it, and read the entry that had been vexing her for the last two centuries.

· · · ·

Target: Holine IV Laerdsfeld, Empress of the Nielda, Supreme Commander of the Joint Armed Forces, and Provider for the Means of Victory.

Time of Death: 15th of Mage, in the 973rd year since the Frost broke, 17:23

Location of Death: The Hearth of Holine IV, Medea

Cause of Death: beaten to death with her own iglakosch

· · · ·

To say that any part of the entry was her style was grossly untrue. She preferred to work in the shadows, unseen and unknown. Targets this high profile, let alone ones killed by such direct and brutal means, were simply not how she preferred to operate. But the book did not like to be ignored, and Rea did not want another divergent event. She'd barely survived the last one, and many of her friends had not.

Then there was the logistical problem of killing the Empress. The full might of the Imperial Guard stood between her and Rea, and that was a very real threat multiplied a hundred times over by the vast array of defensive enchantments, technology, and reality scars present in the palace itself. And even then, she couldn't complete the mission, because it needed to be done in the Hearth. Rea had spent the last two centuries searching for the location of this vault in construction records, equipment manifests, and transport logs. She'd even questioned palace staff and senior officials looking for it. There was no record she had access to. Short of breaking into the physical archives of the Bureau of Records and History's Palace branch, there was no hope of finding it at this point. If she were more of a combatant, she'd probably have tried that too.

Wait. She knew a combat expert. Someone with every reason to hate Holine, to want her dead even. He was right here too.

I thought you were Dead. This is going to be so much easier.

She smiled. This could work.

Chapter Three

In Which A Member Of Her Majesties Armed Forces Is Ejected From The Premises

Krell was confused. What were they talking about? He glanced around, hearing a distant siren. A moment passed. The sound didn't grow any closer before stopping. Streetlamps dimmed as the evening drew on. The little Gascan city carried on as though he had never arrived. Finally, he felt it was safe to reply.

I need to get off world. Can you help me?

He sent the message and waited for a reply. It didn't take long.

Maybe.

And then

I need you to verify a few things first. Why are you alive? Where did you first meet the Emperor? And What is your favorite colour?

His Favorite...What? Krell thought back to whether or not he had set any security questions last time his clearance was upgraded. Even if he hadn't, and he honestly wasn't sure. The answers to nearly all of them had changed. Imperial Blue had taken a far more sinister connotation since his flight.

The Grey of a Taran Fog. The official record states that the Emperor and I met at my promotion to Admiral, though in truth we had been friends since I attended the academy, where we met in Realm. I rescued him from a Dragon that had been provoked by Secloran Saboteurs. Reports of my death are not exaggerated. I am sustained by a foul magic,...

Krell wanted to say that he was cursed, that he sought only to rest. But not yet. Not until Holine was dead. He couldn't let go until she was brought to justice. Until she was brought down.

The work of Holine Laerdsfeld, daughter of the Emperor.

• • • •

Rea nodded grimly. Kate was right, Holine was evil. She'd be graceful about it when she found out, but she'd probably call for action from the Pantheon and the Guard. Raising someone as a sentient undead was distinctly illegal, both for Nielda and also for Immortals. What was more important was that it provided her with a witness to Holine's ability to create an iglakosch. There was no question what she was now, only how to deal with her. As for the rest of his responses, there was no doubt that it was truly the Admiral. All contemporary accounts had painted him as a romantic fucking nerd, and it seemed that death had not erased that aspect of his character, even if circumstances had dimmed his patriotism. A shame, but only for the Empire; He'd be no less effective for its loss, but they'd lost their best, most loyal subject.

Identity confirmed. How urgently do you require transportation?

It was a silly question. The answer was ASAP, but Rea was going to need time to find a destination and the time it took for him to answer was enough for her to locate the next transport to the Imperial Palace. If she could get him there, then he could locate the records she needed. As his reply blipped onto the chat bubble, she reached the bottom of the transport list. All ships headed to the capitol required sealed authorization from an Imperial Noble or Command Councilor.

Damn. She could forge one of course, but she couldn't get it to him without meeting him in person. Besides, the sealing wax was enchanted with the time of sealing for inspection, even with her skills, it would be challenging. It would be easier to find a sympathetic Noble or Traitor General then to steal and use the wax undetected.

I am currently being hunted. Unless you can hide me here until the guard leaves, the sooner the better.

That was an option, if she wanted to buy time. A sighting of the Lich off world could be arranged, and might distract the guard long enough to get him off world before they realized the trick, but then they would be hunting again and there was no guarantee they wouldn't interdict every transport looking for him.

Even then, time was not on her side. She needed to get him to the capitol.

The quickest, safe option is to head to the Capitol, but you will need to forge the mark of a Command Councilor or Imperial Noble. I can provide you with such a forgery, if you can obtain sealing wax undetected. Otherwise, it will take at least a day to arrange travel off world without scrutiny.

It wasn't entirely untrue. She could arrange travel off world in only a few hours, which would technically be tomorrow. But if there was a chance he could go directly to the capitol, that would be easier for her by far, and give her more time to plan the incursion on the Archives. Even just a few days could make all the difference in a situation this complex. Worst case scenario, she'd ask for help. Kate wouldn't like needing to break into the Palace again, but at least this time she wouldn't be killing anyone. Petra on the other hand, she would be pretty unhappy about needing to be involved at all, and the cover-up for that unsubtle, inconsiderate mess would take three decades.

If the reports were to be believed, then this Admiral could best Dragons, Frost Knights, and some of the greatest mortal warriors in the known universe. There was nothing that could stop him.

• • • •

Krell stared at the screen, distressingly aware of his inability to blink. Surely, he was misreading the message. If he could just, focus a little harder, he would be able to read it correctly, rather than seeing this insane request to steal a closely guarded possession from the highest levels of government, in order to escape into the secure heart of his greatest enemy's backyard.

But he could not blink, and so the message continued unchanged. Sealing wax for a forgery so he could escape Gasca bound for the homeworld, such was the request this stranger was making. This was a terrible idea.

That is a terrible plan. The palace of Gasca is too secure for me to enter undetected, and it would be easier to fight my way across the shuttleyard and steal a ship than to face their defenses.

-Every Guardsman on the planet is in the field hunting you, and most of the troops. As long as you can avoid making a ruckus, you could probably make it into the bedchambers of the king before anyone thought twice.

Unless the_Witch knew something about the wards on the palace he didn't, he doubted undead would be able to enter as easily as to simply walk in.

Is there another source of the Sealing Wax? Someone must produce it and enchant it, perhaps we could persuade them to craft some?

-There is. Her name is Atalaine, and she lives on the palace grounds. She's a ninth generation wax-maker and descended from the Royal Family.

And?

-I'll try to get in contact with her while you make your way to the palace. I'm uploading a Transit pass and complete route map to your tablet. Happy Questing!

The pass popped up on screen seconds later, an image of him, identifying him as 'silent phantom J6D-HH8', an entity with full transit privileges. There was even a set of instructions for those checking his information instructing them that he could not respond, and was harmless unless confronted. It had an Imperial Guard sign-off and his file even included a Mystic Experimentation Accident discharge notification indicating that it was unclear which of sixteen fatalities of a military training accident he was, but that his quasi-death had entitled him to veteran tax status and freedom-to-haunt, regardless of which fatality he was. He'd only seen a handful of these as a High Admiral, and was pleasantly surprised to see his own signature on the discharge. Apparently the_Witch had a sense of irony, and he couldn't help but wonder how many other favors he'd unwittingly done for her over the years as he began to drift toward a nearby transit station, catching a three hour early morning hop to the palace garden station. No one bothered him, or even looked at him beyond a cursory glance and his new transit pass seemed to work perfectly. His perception filter held, and this new identity seemed to get him through daily inconveniences without drawing attention. It was uncanny how easy it was to get around this way.

As he stepped off near the Palace Gardens just after sunrise, Krell noticed that there was a squad of troopers checking passes near the garden gates, with a dozen more watching from a camp. They were set up beside a platoon sized transport vehicle on a nearby hillock, which overlooked the small crowd of tourists. Just past the gates was a platoon of Retainers, the private military of the Gascan crown. From the looks of things, the Imperial troopers had been allowed to set up a post at the gate, but been denied access to the palace grounds. There was no Imperial Guard in sight, which was both welcome and unsurprising, given that a full squad should have already been assigned to the palace. More concerning than the Guards most likely stationed here at the palace were the Gascan Royalty. Although the world was known for its cuisine, culture, and cunning, it had only done so through the martial precision and notorious longevity of the ruling Alicean Dynasty, which was second only to the Imperial line in the length of its rule. There was no guarantee that they would be hostile toward him, but Krell wasn't confident he could bypass them without conflict either. This whole adventure was unnecessarily dangerous, but the_Witch seemed to think this was the most effective way for him to get off world. He waited for a moment, habit blowing in the slight breeze that came off the nearby mountains, and let the anxiety of tourists and pilgrims caught in the dual checkpoints refuel his reserve of magical power before he entered the palace.

To Krell's surprise, the Imperial troopers stopped him to run his record. He waited, patiently, while three of them read over his documentation, looking for abnormalities. The retainers seemed to take an interest in his presence, and he saw one of them talk into their wrist as a second tapped his helmet and focused on the Imperial document inspection team. He continued to exercise patience, and found it rewarded as a young woman, wearing a wine-red steelsilk dress with a curved axe at her side approached the gate.

"Lieutenant, what seems to be the hold up?" came a collected voice. "Is there some confusion about this phantom's authorization, or perhaps you need to double check the imperial policy regarding mystic experimentation victims?"

One of the troopers stood and turned with a groan. "Look, your ladyship, we have orders from the Empress to confirm the identity of all non-living entities passing through Imperial checkpoints."

"It's Your Highness, and unless you wish to be reassigned to an asteroid outpost on the border, you'd do well to lose the attitude. I am acquainted with Her Majesty's orders, but if you continue to harass our citizens without cause, then you will leave me no choice but to raise the issue to His Highness, the King." A small crowd began to gather as the princess crossed beyond the threshold of the palace. A few of the queued visitors pulled tablets from pockets and pouches and began recording the interaction. "And frankly, Her Majesty's orders have been erratic of late. Dispatching hundreds of Imperial Guards across our world, entering our homes looking for a supposed Lich, and now posting her troops in front of our Royal Palace. Gasca is perfectly capable of dealing with a foreign agent on its own, and a simple request would have been quite enough."

There was a cheer from the crowd. If Krell had been able to frown, it would have made his current ghastly grin far more indicative of the glee he felt watching this prince-ling exercise her statecraft like this. It was a small moment, but the popular election was decided by the weight of such moments and there was no telling which one would tip things into succession. Judging by the axe at her side though, he suspected that she was fully prepared to act on her feelings if the guards did not comply, and a cold hope beneath his ribs wished that it would come to blows.

"I'll be sure to let her Majesty know that. Now step back into your fancy garden and let me do my job, or I'll have you arrested for obstruction, Your Highness." There were gasps from the crowd, but also a sudden burst of anger as several locals blurted out their feelings on the matter. Krell sighed and prepared to drift through the gate as he saw the other troopers start nervously reaching for their arms, while their retainer counterparts began repositioning to avoid being caught in the open. He made a note that the retainers were forming a perimeter not on the fence, but relative to the Princess, and moved to maintain a similar distance. She, in turn, took a deep breath and closed her eyes.

"Lieutenant, as Seneschal of this palace and her grounds, I must ask you to take your men and leave at once. His Highness' Royal Retainers and I will assume the responsibility of screening visitors, in accordance with Her Majesty's order, from this moment forward. Your services are no longer required."

"I'm not on Palace grounds. These are Her Majesty's lands."

"Maybe on Corek, but not on Gasca. Alicea's treaty, as reaffirmed by Tala the Storm Mage in the time of Hierarchs, clearly defines the royal house as holding the authority to expel any junior officer of the Empire from the planet's soil by verbal request only. Return to your base. I will submit the request to your commander before you arrive and you will be off world by day's end. You are no longer welcome here." There was a cheer from the crowd that covered the lieutenant's response, thankfully. The man turned back toward Krell and motioned for the troopers to arrest him. As they began to move there was a glint of red and Krell found himself staring at the blade of an axe as it spun through the air toward him.

• • • •

"Where is it?"

Rea had accumulated a stunningly large number of things over the years, most of them useful at one point or another. The problem with her collection was that, in spite of having been around longer than any active Imperial warship, and many government offices, she had never really had the time to organize the aforementioned things. Kate had offered to organize them for her on several occasions, but Rea preferred not to let the wizard pour over ten thousand years of forgeries, stolen keys, and broken artifacts. Honestly, it would take Kate half a year just to calm down after discovering some of the documents she assumed were still piled away somewhere. She had learned that when it came to Kate, it was better not to let her find a loose thread, let alone page.

She passed a row of yellowed stacks of loose paper, and turned right at the out-of-tune piano designed to hide a ballista. If she remembered the layout of her private warehouse correctly, then the tools she'd need to forge a ruling noble's signet should be just up ahead, past the obscene statue she'd stolen from the collection of that one art snob back in the 4020s and before the weird shrine to her that the local Medeans had erected as part of construction.

Sure enough, there, atop a monument to some forgotten fae, was a cracked wooden box with an elaborate coat of arms. She felt a pang as she looked down at the intricate details of the royal crest of Anatolia.

For a moment the roar of battle surrounded her as she reached out. She could hear a woman calling out for help as bowstrings twanged and rocks cracked as the steel darts tried to embed themselves in the surrounding canyon. A cheer rose as massive engines roared to life, the first of millions in the years to come as the Empire grew. A man, full grown and wearing a torn cloak, holding out the box to her, bidding her to take it and run. Darkness that shone like a beacon, and that scythe, dripping with ichor as a hearty matron rested her weight on it in the shadow of a towering horned monster while a girl, only a few years older than Rea, mopped her mistress brow.

She wiped a tear from her eye as the memories faded. "Never again." she whispered, reassuring no one.

All set up to forge your documentation. Any idea of when you'll have the wax? She typed, hoping Krell would keep up his end of the arrangement.

-No. I got held up at the gate, but I was able to slip inside.

You got past security? Rea began queuing up security footage for the Gascan palace. It was strange that there would be any security, let alone that they would stop someone with the credentials she'd assigned him.

-Holine posted a group of soldiers at the gate. They had a checkpoint set up and were stopping everyone to check IDs. Luckily, the Seneschal came out and intervened. Rea watched the recording as a modestly dressed young woman walked down from the palace and began speaking with the commander. The two exchanged words for a minute, then he motioned to his men to arrest the skeletal figure in the habit she mentally noted as being Krell. No sooner had he motioned than did the lady whip the axe from her side across the checkpoint, pinning the manacles to a nearby tree. The troopers began drawing their weapons and a group of retainers on the other side of the gate quickly loosed a volley of pulse fire into the checkpoint, disarming several of the Imperial soldiers and driving the rest into cover. The lady, likely a princess, Rea suspected, charged at the officer, axe snapping back into her hand. As the melee began to unfold and Krell silently drifted through the combat zone onto palace grounds, Rea saw the familiar disappointment of a pair of crackling eyes in her mind. As the group of troopers began to fall back, the princess was hot on their heels, and the stormy eyes in Rea's memory gave way to another, a bared throat and a head thrown back toward the sky as rolling laughter gave way to a joyous howl. Rea flagged the footage for the Gascan news networks, and noted that the Princess's ancestor would be exceedingly proud of her legacy.

She'll make a good Queen someday. Keep me posted.

Chapter Four

In Which Art Is Appreciated And Something Important Falls From A Shelf

The Royal Palace of Gasca wasn't even in the same league as the Imperial Palace. There was no comparing the automated defenses, the redundant barracks control centers, the layer after layer of wards and traps of the Imperial Palace to the beauty of Gasca's Royal Palace. The innermost gardens were said to have been planted by Alicea I herself, and successive generations had only expanded on her work. Groves of trees from across the Empire were scattered throughout the kilometers of public trails, themselves twisting around sculptures by some of the Empire's most prominent artists and crossing canals and ponds on scenic bridges. Flowers in every colour imaginable were planted in carefully planned beds to form living paintings. In the distance were greenhouses designed to protect and nurture plants not suited to the local climate. It was not Krell's first visit to the pride of Gasca, but each time was as breathtaking as the last, a fact saddened by his now longstanding incapacity for breath.

The palace proper was built against the side of a mountain, and stretched out before him like a small town. The main building was three stories, with towers that rose to six, but there were several buildings around it that formed a perimeter. These buildings formed an interlocking maze and served as storehouses and barracks for Gasca's Retainers and servants. There was, when last he was privy to such details, beds for ten thousand although only about a thousand or so, they had promised, were for warriors. He'd never trusted that figure, but trusted them well enough not to abuse their private army.

The main path passed through a massive work of art designed to flank the stairs leading to the front door of the palace. The ancient mosaic was said to depict the first legendary battle for Gasca, in which Alicea dueled a Ga-Vok shaman. On one side stood Alicea with one of her legendary axes in one hand and a fistful of lightning in the other. Behind her, trailing down the stairs were Nieldic soldiers, garbed in the armor of the early colonial era, against a backdrop of a small mountain fortress and leaves blown in from a nearby forest. On the other was a powerfully built Ga-Vok wielding an axe and calling lightning of her own. Behind the warlock was a tribe of the lupine Ga-Vok, their fangs bared and snouts angled downward as they bore their axes up the stairs toward a fortress, river rapids boiling behind them. The details of the battle had been lost to history, but the mosaic had been erected during Alicea's life to commemorate the events leading to her rise to power. There had been an ostensibly non-fiction book published not long ago that cast the events depicted into question, but the historical community had widely disregarded the book as poorly researched historical fantasy. Still, it had caused quite a stir when several members of the Ga-Vok council of elders had come forward to express that their oral histories supported the account of Alicea having been one of the silver-slain.

Beyond the entrance, much of the palace remained open to the public. The walls were adorned with the finest portraits and landscapes, and a station staffed with a dozen guides advertised tours of the galleries. Krell had no need for a guide. He'd memorized the layouts of all of the royal palaces as a part of his responsibilities as High Admiral. The difference in defensive strategies provided a useful base for understanding the inclinations of the noble houses. Gasca was known for a willingness to meet enemies in the field, and the security of their palace reflected a sentiment that an enemy who had reached so deep into their territory was one who had already defeated them. It made for a beautiful palace, but not a defensible one. This worked out in his favor now, as he did not need to worry about patrols or automated defenses. Gasca's reputation for open-mindedness also served him well, as he didn't need to worry about setting off any wards by simply existing as a Lich. It was honestly refreshing, not needing to constantly scan for some hidden sigil or glyph that would attempt to blast him into the afterlife or let loose a horrific wail to alarm every guard in a ten kilometer radius.

The Royal Enchanter's Tower was on the west-northwestern corner of the palace, through a locked gate on the side of a patio with an elaborate fountain by Horence of Kraina depicting four water nymphs frolicking around a terrified sailor. The detailed musculature of the sailor was quite good, and the lock was warded against attempts to open it by magic.

Any chance you can open a door for me?

There was a clicking sound, and the gate swung open as he finished typing. Krell glanced around him, trying to pinpoint the security cameras she must have used to spot him, before realizing that she'd probably been tracking the tablet itself. It was far from a relief, but at least it meant he wasn't being spied on. He stepped through and found himself in a small yard full of obscure herbs. Across this yard was the tower itself, and there at the door was a blind woman with a staff.

"Hello Admiral. I was notified you would be coming. Please, come in?"

• • • •

"Atalaine, I presume?" Krell asked as he drifted up the stairs behind the blind enchantress.

"The same. It's a bit of a surprise to find trouble of your magnitude on my doorstep, but no matter." She turned at the top of the curving narrow path that lead up the tower. "Not the first time I've had a wanted man on my docket for the day." Then she tapped the door with the whorled end of her staff, and the door swung open invitingly.

It was expected of an Enchanter's space that they be larger within than without, but Atalaine had broken from tradition. The room was little more than a private study, the walls lined with interestingly shaped jars, each in their own cubby. In the center of the fairly clean room was a circular platform that rose a few centimeters from the floor, engraved with a series of permanent unmarked circles. Across from the door was a small desk with a few neatly placed implements. The ceiling was domed, and a number of herbs had been hung to dry toward the edges, where they could be easily reached from the floor. Krell noticed that every bunch of herbs was suspended from a ribbon, and weighed down by an ornate metal trinket.

Atalaine was plainly dressed. She wore a soft grey dress that came to her ankles, and a heavy apron stained by chalk, incense, and ash. Her head was shaved, but the roots showed the sort of white that only age could dye. Her wrinkles spoke of joy, and the shallow scars scattered across her forearms spoke of experience in her craft. For the first time in a century, Krell felt the satisfaction of knowing that the people he had sworn to protect those long years ago were still safe. But as he thought of Holine's plots, the moment soured. This should have been his retirement, had she not...

"I have a message here," She tapped a tablet on her desk, "Authorizing you a single wax seal." She slid open a drawer and set a small paper package on the desk.

"Yes, I need passage off world, and no one is permitted to leave without authorization."

"Indeed. Apparently, they are trying to catch someone. Someone with powerful connections, who cannot teleport far enough to leave the planet, and who is enough of a threat that the Imperial Guard has been dispatched all across the world."

There was a terrible pause. 'kill her!' cried out a dark and fearful power within him, but Krell stifled the lich.

"You seem remarkably calm for someone face to face with a Lich," Krell said.

"My old professor back at the academy made sure her students were prepared to handle anything we encountered. If I die, at least they can tell my father I died well." She grinned, gripping her staff firmly. "But, discretion is the better part of valor, and it takes more than a steady hand and the ability to draw a perfect circle to get a cushy job like this one. Where are you going from here? Will you continue to run?"

"It's been suggested that I head to the Capitol. From there I do not know."

The old woman lifted the lump of wax, or at least that's what Krell presumed was in the bundle of paper. She handled it carefully, the paper crinkling audibly. "It would be treason to give you this."

"If you'd like, I could knock you out? I promise to make it as painless as possible."

Atalaine laughed loudly for nearly a minute before coughing. "I appreciate the offer, but I'd rather not." She sighed, then set the package down on the desk. "My father, Athalion, and the other nobles have been called to the capitol. The rumors say that they are deliberating regarding war with Seclora."

Krell did not think he could have despised the Empress more, and yet again she had found a way. Seclora was an incredibly powerful nation, with a fleet to rival the Nielda's own and armies well exceeding their numbers. It was a fool's quest for glory, and would lead only to ruin. Popular support was not behind her, yet, but it was growing by the year. She knew not to move now, She wasn't incompetent. So why would she be holding a vote?

"His Highness believes she is trying to identify which of the nobles will support her warmongering. He set his affairs in order before departing, and left all of the house's greatest heirlooms behind. But I am not sure the Empress would be so rash as to attack her own nobles."

Krell reached into his habit and lifted the locket that still hung atop his bare ribs. The picture of Kevand at his wedding had aged though not to the point of being unrecognizable, and there was no forgetting the cheeky grin that looked back at him from his beloved Penalupa. 'May your bonds be as unbreakable as your spirit, High Admiral ~K&P' Krell shut it forcefully and looked back to Atalaine.

"Then your father is in grave danger. Holine feels no loyalty to anyone, not her nobles, not her own family, not even the Empire itself. Please, I know how terrible a thing I am asking of you, but I need that wax."

The Enchantress shrank back. "And then what?"

Krell straightened to his full height, lifting higher still into the air. "And then I will uphold my Oath, and protect the people of the Empire from those who would threaten them." The fire within his vacant skull flared a deep, metallic blue, "I swear to you, that I will face Holine, and save your father!"

Behind him, a sharp clack broke the moment. The blood red staff of an Imperial guard was unmistakable in the hand of an armored figure at the top of the stairs. "Then you will die first, Traitor!"

• • • •

Krell drifted in front of Atalaine as he moved to the center of the round tower room. There was little space to maneuver, but it seemed unlikely that his success with previous Guardsmen would carry. "Holine has betrayed the most sacred laws of the Empire. It is not treason to defend the lives of its citizens against her."

"It is not for you to decide, rebel." the guard spat. Even through the modulator that ensured all members of the Guard spoke with the same voice, Krell could hear the youth and confidence of his apparent adversary. The young guard had probably been brought up under Holine's rule and fallen for the propaganda.

"Please understand," Krell began, but the guard slung a burst of flame with an upward strike from his staff and quickly began to follow up with a second. He deflected the blast toward a the stone arches of the ceiling and lunged forward to counter the second, blocking the staff and dispersing the gathering flame.

Instinctively, Krell found a burst of heat forming in his hand, bidden by the lich. He fought back the urging voice and strained to withhold the power to destroy as he drove his skeletal fist toward the guard's midsection. He felt his hand stretching out as the breastplate turned his blow aside, the space between bones expanding as knuckles fought friction to keep up with his wrist. Krell knew that the enchanted armor would surely be too resistant for such a mundane attack to be effective, but it was better than unleashing a magical attack in such a delicate workspace. The lich growled at his feeble efforts, and continued to pry at his self-control.

He'd sparred with guardsmen in the past, but an actual fight was an experience he'd generally managed to avoid. They were among the best equipped warriors in the universe, with the training and magical potency to match. In his current state, Krell was faced with a serious challenge if he wanted them both to walk away from this fight intact. He rolled to the side, dodging the red blur from an overhead strike that cracked the stones of the floor. Again he quelled the instinct, catching himself as he began to pull a spike of stone and dust from the floor beneath his assailant.

"I don't wish to fight you." Krell thrust himself backward out of the way of a sweeping strike, only the speed of his movement betrayed the intentionality of his action through his ever-present levitation. He quickly caught a jagged shard of ice that followed the strike, absorbing the magic that had coalesced it into his own. The guard lunged forward with a series of wide swings, driving Krell back into a cabinet. There was a sound of shattered glass as something fell to the ground, and Krell darted aside as he smelled some sort of gas emitting from the shelf behind him. He heard wood crack as a final blow impacted against the cabinet itself, and Krell spun to face the guard. Suddenly he was knocked several inches to his side as the staff, rebounding off of the damaged cabinet, from which bottles now fell to the floor below, collided with his arm. It lacked the force to cause real damage, but caught him off guard never the less.

"Wait, look out!" came a woman's voice behind him as the guard scraped his staff along the ground. Tongues of flame were quickly begining to pour from a cracked bottle nearby. As the staff came forward, then upward toward Krell, he saw a mote of silver flame shoot forth from the bottle. He rushed to shield Atalaine as he saw the flames alight on the circle engraved into the center of the room.

There was a sound like a curtain ripping, and several of the fallen components turned to vapor as the floor fell from reality and the room filled with the roar of flame. Krell desperately formed a barrier as a porcine being with skin like embers burst into the tower from beyond.

Stone shattered, his shield faltered, and Krell fell for a moment before hovering to a stop amidst the ruined tower. A massive, tusked man covered in bristles of silver and smelling of brimstone and incense now stood in its place. Krell spotted movement across the ruin, and saw the guard emerge beneath some rubble, bloodied but armed. The boar-man began to bellow with laughter and smoke.

"Urun, the Argent Flame walks the world once more! Woe befall those who bound him so long ago!" The guard, ignoring the three story elemental with pecs the size of windows and shoulders like a carpet, began to dash across the yard toward Krell, hurling chunks of rubble across the ruins with telekinetic force. As he began to dodge the projectiles, Krell spotted a bit of grey fabric under a nearby stone.

"Atalaine!" He shouted as he extended his power and disintegrated stone after stone, furiously excavating the fallen enchantress. He could feel what little life remained fading as he pulled her bent and torn body from under her ruined home. He desperately reached for the familiar power he'd wielded with such ease so long ago, but could not find the power to mend her wounds within his undead essence.

"S-s-saav.."

"Hold on. Help will come. Hold on a little longer."

Atalaine reached up, her blood visibly struggling to hold what remained of her together. Nielda were hard to kill, but even bones of steel and symbiotic blood couldn't prevent organ failure from being scorched and crushed when half a tower fell on you.

"Faath-er?" He felt her body giving way under the strain of the damage. He tried to wrest control of her body, hold it together just a little longer, tendrils of deathly energy seeping from him and holding her together. She was too broken to survive, but what life she had left was anathema to such necrotic animus. There was no magic he could use, no matter how hard he tried, that could save her.

"I'm so sorry Atalaine. I swear I'll save your father, by blood and bone." She nodded, grimacing through the pain as the life left her. Krell felt, for a brief moment, as her spirit left and he felt her power joining with his own, his sorrow was rapidly overcome by the twisted joy of power as the lich burst from its mental cage. His body lifted into the air, surging with the noble servant's magic, and he let her bones roll from his hands as he turned to face the guard behind him. Urun had them aloft, and seemed to have the upper hand. The guard drove their staff into the elemental's fist, a spike of ice driving into its wrist. As steam erupted from the wound, he pushed free and began to twist in the air so he could land on his feet.

The lich caught up with him halfway to the ground, a single, bony finger outstretched. The guard gasped, and he drove that fearful exhalation into him like an inferno, consuming enchantments and wards alike in a burst of heat so that only ashes met the ground. He drifted downward, half a meter off the ground even after that display of power, and faced the elemental.

Chapter Five

In Which Persons With Large Swords Feature Prominently

Forgery was not at the top of Rea's list of preferred activities, but the advantages of experience and extensive access to Imperial databases did make it a fairly straightforward one. She double checked the protocol being used to access the homeworld, pulled up the appropriate form, and traced over an earlier version of the authorization she had written in the past in the stylized Anatolian script that belonged to her particular seal.

In practice, Anatolia had not been a part of the Nieldic Empire in nearly six thousand years. Rea could no more forget the events of that week than she could the rest of that lost century, but to most the Shade Invasion was a decade of horror and wrath that ended with the death of Anatolia's star and the twisting of her flora and fauna into hostile forms. The vile miasma that infected the whole of that world had resulted in a quarantine so thorough that most navigational computers and charts had been deliberately rewritten to hide its existence and prevent even an accidental arrival within the system. Rea had not been consulted on the project, but she had certainly approved of it.

In technicality, there was no system to revoke the status of a world as belonging to a major noble. Tradition considered it to be a high honor and even as Anatolia was concealed from the public behind legends of its destruction, its chair and seal remained in the bureaucracy of the Empire. And so, as the last remaining member of the royal bloodline of Anatolia, more unfathomably distant than most would even dream of, Rea was in her full legal rights to authorize Krell's travel.

Of course, Rea thought, as she added a flourish to the handwritten document that would soon be placed into a scanner for review by a program built on an operating system she had compromised from its very conception, it was quite illegal for an imperial official to be immortal. Had she ever been issued an Imperial Guard bodyguard detail, it would be their responsibility to execute her for the crime of non-mortality. This meant that the document she held was not so much criminal, as were the hands that held it. A mischievous grin crept over her as she considered her own legality.

"Rea. Why is there a Lich mourning Atalaine?" came a woman's voice from the balcony, its glass door sliding quickly open. Heavy bootfalls filled the air as an imposing woman in polished plate strode across the room, unrelenting and swift. Polite as well, as evidenced by how gently the door slid closed behind her.

"Hello Petra. Are you asking me as the professor or the paladin?" Rea dotted an ' I ' with a careful down-stroke.

"That's..." She gathered herself, exhaling slowly. "It depends on your answer." Delicately filigreed gauntlets were replaced by calloused hands as the woman began to dismiss pieces of armor until only her void-dark sword remained. She loomed over Rea as she leaned into the desk on a single clenched fist.

"Admiral Casat is there retrieving sealing wax so he can get passage to the palace." She blew gently on the letter before turning to face the stern warrior standing over her shoulder. "I don't know why he's mourning her, you'd need to ask him."

Petra stood back upright, sighing and muttering. Rea had been invited to some of the funerals Petra had attended. The professor had never forgotten any of her students, even after all her years in teaching. She'd never accept it, but she'd inherited her mother's keen memory for the lost.

After a moment, Petra recovered from her allowance of grief, and resumed her interrogations. "There is a Fire Elemental Prince in the middle of the courtyard."

"I'm sure they'll handle it. Gasca's retainers are very capable."

"Are you going to do anything about it?"

"I'm going to meet him at the port to give him his authorization to travel and explain to him how he can pay me back."

Petra grabbed a chair from the dining table and sat down next to Rea's desk facing her. "Does he know he's going to be paying you?"

Rea thought for a moment. She couldn't remember whether or not she'd mentioned it. His reputation was honest enough it had never really occurred to her that he might not agree to her terms. He wasn't in a situation to say no either way, but asking was clearly the right thing to do.

"No, I haven't asked him yet."

"Rea."

"I know! I should ask first before I make anyone do things."

"Rea," Petra's voice softened, "You shouldn't be making people do things at all."

"I know."

There was a pause. Rea didn't want to turn around, but she knew Petra was still behind her like a shadow.

"I see Kate dropped by. She's a sweet girl."

"She's been bringing me groceries."

"About how long do you think she's been doing that?" Petra inquired.

"Since the war ended probably. Where are you going with this?"

"You need to get out of the house, Rea. Meet people, form attachments, stop hiding and start living!" Petra gestured widely as she pontificated. Rea picked up her coffee, held it up, and shook it meaningfully. "No, Rea, ordering overpriced drinks is not meeting people. I mean you've got to put yourself out there. Who have you spoken with in the past decade that wasn't Kate or I?"

"Zee..."

"ZeeGee doesn't count." Petra bristled. The taller woman rose, elements of armor bursting into the air around her like fireworks and quickly securing themselves to her body. "Get ahold of me before your next target. I expect you to tell me someone's name and something you couldn't have learned about them from a file or you need to spar with me again."

"Ugh! Fine." Rea replied as Petra vanished. She carefully folded the letter and placed it and her seal into a hidden pocket in her bag. She had to meet Krell at the port in a few hours, assuming that elemental didn't delay him much longer.

· · · ·

The Lich faced the colossal being that stood in the heart of the rubble, whose amusement was visible even through the heat that warped the air around him. An icy lance formed in its hand, and launched forward through a series of arcane circles like a railgun round before evaporating three feet away from Urun's glistening hide. The elemental stretched out his hand and a jet of blue-white flame nearly carved Krell in half. The now burning habit was discarded; a Lich had no such mortal concerns. An incantation drew up a corona of chilled air to reduce the heat of future blasts, and a twisting gesture created an unseen barrier that interposed itself between it and the elemental. A molten stone impacted the barrier even as it formed, half splattering to the ground while the rest slid heavily off the phantasmal cover.

Krell was once again a passenger in his own body. He quickly began to gather his faculties and to test all his senses. He could still feel the heat of his surroundings, smell the sulfurous air, and sense the incredible reserve of power the Lich now wielded. Atalaine's spirit had been strong. Between her and the late guardsman, there was an abundance of power now available. Krell was adrift in the fear of their last moments, and what little life he had was all but drowned out by the power of unlife now steering him.

"A mere Lich is no match for a Prince of Flame. Give up now," taunted Urun from atop a pile of stone that was, relative to the normal melting speed of stone at least, melting rapidly. "All I ask is to consume this tower in which I have been held against my will. Give me this act of retribution and I will leave willingly."

"No" replied the Lich, as a cascade of arcane bolts swirled forth from the space around his hand, each one leaving a small dark spot on Urun. Krell, however, considered the request. The elemental had not attacked him when he had retreated from it, nor had it made any effort to destroy Atalaine or reveled in her death. It clearly had some motivation beyond mere destruction, and if he could regain control of his body, perhaps he could negotiate.

"Fool! Would you deny me even so simple a request? Very well then." He plunged a hand into the ground and drew a dripping crescent blade of molten earth. "I shall burn your impurity from this world also." The Lich vanished as the blade swept across the courtyard, leaving a glowing scar in the columns behind it. As it reformed on a nearby rooftop, it unleashed a bolt of energy toward the silver tusked elemental. Urun parried, and the blade cracked in half, falling to the ground with a crash. He snorted, sheathed the ruined weapon to the hilt in the ground, and drew it anew, lunging forward. Again the Lich vanished, appearing 20 meters away. But this time, as it appeared it was snatched up in the hand of the boar-man and held aloft in a smoldering grip.

Krell could feel his bones heating in Urun's grip, but even through the pain he sensed the Lich's rage. The power waned with every spell, and Krell could feel desperation beginning to spark in dark entity. The Lich willed himself out of Urun's grip, exerting its power to bend space and vanish once more, and Krell used the moment to press against his captor. He felt the locket hanging within his chest. He thought of Penalupa's coy smile, and of the feeling of Kevand's hand on his shoulder. He saw a sea stretched out before him, still as glass, and found the strength to stand against the Lich. Then, he dug into that reserve of power for Atalaine's devotion to her own family, and he pushed it into every atom of his skeletal form. The oath of office coursed through his thoughts, pounding the Lich's influence over him until it began to retreat. Krell appeared on the ground before Urun, and he took a knee.

"Forgive me," he shouted, "I am Krell Casat, and I have not yet surrendered to the Lich within me. I accept your terms, and cede the ruins of this tower to your wrath." The glowing blade halted centimeters from his head. "It is a travesty to see one of your stature bound. Please, if you would, tell me how it is that you have been abused in this manner, that I may help bring your captor to justice."

Urun's blade lowered, collapsing into a formless mass of lava as he dropped it to the ground. "You are still able to seize control? I have never met one such as you." He stroked the mass of silver bristles that protruded from the back of his neck. "I was summoned by a warrior like the one you slew, in another place in your world. They locked me in a jar, sealed by some enchantment. I have watched from that shelf for a hundred years, and swore that if I were ever able to break free, I would ensure that none of my people should ever again see that place." He buried his hands into the rubble, and began to stir it into a pool of molten rock. Bright colors and unearthly sounds emitted from the ruins as the enchanter's tower dissolved into a single igneous mass.

"Thank you, Krell Casat, I will not forget your compassion. Call me if you need me," and the elemental submerged into the brimstone depths, which hardened as he departed for home.

· · · ·

Krell stared breathlessly at the ruins before him, the grey robed skeleton beside him, and the nearly unscathed palace around him. In the absence of combat, he began to recognize the sounds nearby, feet on tiled floors and gasps of disbelief. One set of feet, falling heavily and moving across both garden and paving-stone, was closing quickly, and he turned to see the Seneschal from the gate, a splatter of blood dripping from her axe.

"What happened here?"

Krell paused. His perception filter should have kept her from noticing him. He glanced down, seeing the ring, soot stained but still functional, securely on his finger. He also saw the glint of the locket and a few scraps of charred cloth clinging to his hips and joints where they'd fallen as the habit had burned away. There were a lot of things you could hide by making someone seem less noteworthy, but a lone skeleton hovering amid the debris of an elemental's wrath was not one of them.

"It would seem that a member of the Imperial Guard imprisoned a fire elemental and hid him in your enchanter's tower. I'm afraid Atalaine was caught in the crossfire."

"No. That's..." She teared up, but quickly took a moment to compose herself. "Are you the Lich being sought by Her Majesty's order?"

The Lich surged at the recognition, clawing at his mind to ready for battle. Krell pushed it down with a chuckle, "Don't you think that's a bit of a loaded question? Either I affirm your suspicions and am subject to your judgment, or I deny them and am judged a liar."

"So you do not deny it?" He saw her adjust her grip on the axe. She's readying for battle, crept the Lich.

"I am Krell Casat," he affirmed, defying the nameless evil. "Of late, High Admiral of His Majesty's Imperial Navy, friend to Emperor Kevand the Fourth, and husband to Penalupa."

"Admiral Casat who defeated the Frost Knight of Cariol?" Her hand relaxed, the axe slipping low in her grip. "The Admiral Casat who fought alongside Queen Laen in the Echthebaal Traverse?"

Krell's smile was both grim and perpetual, but in this moment it was also earnest. "The very same."

"Queen Laen was my great-grandmother. She passed thirty summers ago. She complained often that the Imperial Navy's budget would never have been permitted to bloat so much under your guidance."

"It's good to hear that she took my advice to heart. I have wondered if our arguments were worth the years I spent on them." He lowered himself as near to the ground as he could. "I am sorry to hear of her passing. She was a capable leader."

"She was. My grandfather works very hard to live up to her example." She looked down at the skeleton beside them. "The whole family does."

"Atalaine told me that His Highness has been called to the palace to demonstrate his loyalty to Holine."

"Her Majesty wants war with Seclora. My grandfather will never approve of such a waste of lives and resources."

"And she will retaliate against him and see him replaced by whichever of your aunts and uncles will be most pliant to her will."

The woman nodded. "It's no secret here. But Gasca cannot become the birthplace of rebellion again. The Hierarchs are long dead, but never forgotten." She sighed. "So we wait for the people's champion to undo her wickedness and hope to endure this."

Krell had been around nobles long enough to know when he was being played. He was no hero; he was a soldier. He had the motive to undo her, but not the means or the opportunity. No army could storm the Imperial Palace, and only one mage had ever been able to pierce its wards. He was no Arcania. He wasn't even a proper mage any more, just a set of bones and memories.

"I am trying to reach the Homeworld. I came here to get sealing wax, so I could forge documents to slip off world. I doubt any survived..." He gestured to the cooling volcanic stone nearby.

"I can provide you with the wax, but His Highness has the signet. I'll have the servants leave it with some clothes suitable for you and whatever else you might need at the foot of the Wolf."

"Thank you. I am not the champion you seek, but I hope I can at least prepare the way for whoever is."

She tied a cover to the blade of her axe and hung it from her belt. "Respectfully, I look forward to seeing you prove yourself wrong, and when I'm queen, I'm going to need you to come back here and apologize." She whispered into her wrist for a moment, and then gave him a once over before whispering again.

"We'll have your things by the Wolf in twenty. The Guards are on their way over now, so I'd prefer you get going."

"Thank you for everything."

"I look forward to welcoming you back some day for a feast in your honour. Godspeed Mister Casat." And he took his cue to drift away, as fast as his form would allow.

        # Chapter Six

In Which Thing Calm Down Somewhat And A Man Is Reminded To Mind His Own Business

Rea did not like to go out in public. This was not to say she had the slightest difficulty leaving her apartment, which she did at least once a day, but rather that she did not like to be seen. Years of living had taught her that once you were in an open space, you were only as safe as you were aware, and there was nowhere she was more aware than in her chair. From there she commanded a network of cameras, the collective knowledge of a civilization, and an army of unwitting analysts and bureaucrats. From the terminal of the spaceport in Gasca, she was a child with a pair of eyes. Well trained, certainly, experienced beyond measure even, but still only eyes.

And then there was the risk of being discovered. She'd made her fair share of enemies, and some of them were even still active. A crowd of a thousand wasn't certain to contain a shade, but one in ten was far more concerning than she'd prefer to risk. The Pantheon was just as much of a threat. Tala's guidance council had long since become one of Rea's greatest nuisances. Given their competing interests, regulating immortals and limiting immortality, it was somewhat frustrating that the Storm Mage hadn't considered it before enacting her plan. Death guide her, considerate had never been one of Tala's finer qualities. Now, the misguided old fools were as likely to interfere with Rea's work as they were to debate their role in Post-Dark Lady Gravagan cultural development, which is to say regularly.

It was terribly risky. Still, Admiral Casat was her best bet to retrieve the location of Holine's Hearth. She couldn't just walk in, even with all of her magic and technology. The simple fact was that children were not allowed to access the Imperial Palace Analog Archive, even after all she had done for the Empire she was still, and ever had been, a child.

-I have the wax. Alarms may have been raised in the process, but the Nobility seems inclined to assume responsibility for damages.

That's unfortunate. Meet me at the shuttle terminal outside Martessa.

She thought for a moment about what Petra had said, and added,

I have a service to request of you in payment for passage. We can discuss the terms of the service at the terminal. If you're not interested, I'll let you walk away without prejudice.

-I was wondering where the catch would be. I should forewarn you that my soul is not presently available for trade.

Lucky for her, she wasn't interested in trading in souls just yet.

Rea opened her closet. Considering the size of her apartment, her closet was actually quite large. She didn't keep much in it, just a couple of essential outfits and her day to day clothing. For a situation like this one, it would have to be her armor though.

She started with a layer of light padding, more for comfort than protection. After this came her breastplate, a single piece of molded hide that shielded her against nearly all forms of deliberate harm. Then she strapped on a pair of greaves that ensured she landed on her feet while also absorbing the force of any impact, an effect she'd found as useful for blocking low blows as in preserving her from long falls. After that was her bracers, which projected a barrier of force to deflect physical attacks or block magical ones. Then she wrapped herself from head to toe in roll after roll of grey steel-silk, spun by the spiders first bred a thousand years before she was born, the greatest product of a foolish mage. Besides concealing her identity, the wraps gave her ample room to hide paper talismans, engraved runestones, finely inked scrolls, and all manner of vials, each shielded from wayward blows and wandering eyes by the incredibly durable cloth. Lastly she strapped on her aviator's cap, a fashionable accessory, with goggles that would allow her to pierce through all but the most cunning of illusions.

Petra had a policy against charging for her work. Even for Rea, who remembered when they had been the same age, it was unknowable whether she had learned this from her angelic mother, caring father, or simply arrived at it of her own accord. Even without receipts, however, Rea knew that the value of the artistry, to say nothing of the potent enchantments, was enough to equip a dozen Imperial Guards. She set a few herbs on a burner and recited an invocation to hide the strength of the magic from prying eyes, then wiped the ashes over herself to obscure the value of her apparel. A sooty, bandaged child with thick goggles stared back at her from the mirror, only her hands and a few stray tufts of hair showed as she closed the closet doors. She turned and walked to the door.

She paused as she reached the door. Her hand rested on the brass handle.

"Shuttle terminal, Martessa on Gasca. If you'd please?"

The door cracked open of its own accord. The sounds of a crowd came through now. She could hear the footsteps of a thousand people on tile, the boarding calls over an intercom, and smell sweet, burnt herbs, most likely from the soot she'd covered herself in. Rea took a deep breath, pulled the door open toward her, and stepped out into the world.

· · · ·

Krell lacked the breath with which to sigh in exasperation, and yet, by the power of the forbidden magic binding him to existence, sigh he did. The_Witch needed him to perform a service. It wasn't so much the idea that he had more to do in order to earn his freedom as it was that he had really hoped that the effort of getting the wax would be service enough to justify the assistance. Based on the size, he doubted it would be fully spent on a single document. What more could the highest level admin on the net want?

The palace staff generally ignored him as they bustled about their day. It was actually quite impressive to see how faithfully they kept to their work given the altercation at the gate and the destruction of the enchantment tower. Under the circumstances, a bit of panic would have been understandable, but there was none. He could feel the Lich's disappointment, and a weak push to intimidate a particularly worried looking older gardener.

As he approached the steps he saw a handful of well dressed, but somewhat incredulous servants standing at the top.

"I wonder why she wanted them just set out like that?"

"Probably for her brother. You know how he likes to sleep in the outer grounds and 'commune with nature.'"

"Might be she had someone over and they had to leave in a hurry." The young man speaking was lightly smacked on the padded shoulder of his white suit by a woman in a khaki apron with a set of keys hanging from her elbows.

"Shame on you, Her Highness would never be so rude," she huffed, "Or so crass. She's a lady."

"You would know, wouldn't you. Always flirting with that huskarl from the southpost."

"Ceorla's my wife, Gennedy. Of course I flirt with her. Stop policing other people's fun."

"Shove off."

"Hush, Both of you!" rejoined the first servant, a greying man with a well starched surcoat and a metal prosthesis surrounding a green glass eye, "If you're not going to wait quietly for our guest, then leave and let me do so in peace."

So they were waiting for him. Granted, it was an unusual situation and they could hardly be blamed for curiosity, yet he would prefer not to have further witnesses to his passing. There was no reason to risk their lives in the event Holine sent an inquisitorial squad this way while hunting for him.

"Ho there stranger. Do you need anything?" the elder servant called out, his prosthetic eye locked firmly on Krell. 'Kill them!' came the Lich's call, and a momentary tongue of flame quickly turned to smoke as Krell reasserted himself.

"If you are prepared to risk helping an old soldier with neither wealth nor friends, then perhaps I might have some clothes and a place to change?"

"But of course!" replied the woman, nudging the boy and pointing him toward the pile of clothes sitting at the base of the steps. He ran down, swept up the pile of brown cloth, and returned at a stride in only two steps.

"Did her highness send you?" Gennedy asked as he offered the messy pile of clothes.

"Yes, but not as she sent you, I think. She has been gracious, but my travels must continue. Where should I...?"

The man led them to a small gallery, covered from wall to wall in fine paintings of men and women. Nearly every painting was only a little smaller than the palm of his hand, and a few were larger. Each one was in a plain silver frame, adorned only by a single axe carved into the bottom of the frame. There were thousands of portraits, and only a few were younger than Krell himself.

"I apologize if it seems a little poignant, but this is the memorial gallery," said the man.

"There's a painting here for every retainer that died protecting the palace," the woman added.

"That wall over there," the boy said as he pointed to the furthest wall with the worst lighting, "is said to be just the retainers who tried to stop Tala the Storm Mage when she came to depose her father." From the stories Krell had heard of the Storm Mage, he was inclined to believe only about 70% of the densely populated wall was her direct work. She was, after all, also a notoriously talented field commander.

"We'll wait outside," the woman concluded, shooing the boy out as the man waited, his hand on the doorknob.

"Godspeed traveler."

Krell pulled the plain brown robe over his head. Then, he cinched the plain belt sewn into the waist. Lastly, he tried his best to tie the shoes tight enough to keep them on his bare, flesh-less feet. It was a kind gesture, but society did not produce clothes for the dead. No matter how hard he tried, he could never be more than a foreigner in the land of the living, as alien as a Ga-Vok or Harakai. Someday, he hoped to find his pyre and make his way to wherever he belonged.

Chapter Seven

In which public transportation is used, a shoe is nearly lost, and much is revealed to few

The ornate gates to the Royal Palace Gardens were open, and a handful of pilgrims and vacationers passed in and out without incident. A pair of retainers flanked the intricately crafted metal, weapons securely sheathed and holstered, while a full squad worked carefully loading the equipment Krell recognized as parts of the Imperial checkpoint that had greeted him earlier in the day. There were no bodies, but only half of the Imperial troopers he'd seen were currently assisting the retainers in loading their transport. Judging by the bloodstains on the ornamental grasses lining the path that lead up from the transit station, the rest had likely fled.

"Pardon me sir, weren't you here earlier when the Seneschal ejected the commander of this unit?" Krell floated to a stop as one of the retainers, a young woman with a sword at her side, wearing a silvered helm shaped like a serving bowl, and equipped with a Ga-Vok made shield bracer, held out her hand.

"I was. Do you need me to provide a statement?"

"Not at the moment, but if you have a chance to submit a report through the Bureau I'm sure Her Highness would appreciate the support." The woman straightened up and took off her helmet. She bared her throat and held the helmet to her chest as she continued. "I just wanted to say we're terribly sorry for the disruption to your visit. You have our sincerest apologies. Please let us know if there's anything we can do to make it up to you."

"Oh no, I'll be okay. I hope none of your men were injured on my account?"

"Nothing that won't buff out sir!" she replied cheerfully, bringing her head back down to meet his eyes. He could see her tighten her lips, but her cheeks were too high and bright to mistake the smile.

"Are you expecting a visitor?"

"No," her eyes flicked over him searchingly.

"I apologize. It's none of my business. Thank you so much for your hospitality."

"Come back any day you like. After today, I'd bet Her Highness would give you a tour of the grounds herself if you'd like."

"Maybe some day I will take her up on that offer. Take care!" She put her helmet back on and it spun on her head for a moment as it re-secured itself to some mechanism under her coif. He could feel her gaze linger as he wafted down the path.

Gasca was playing host to Ga-Vok diplomats; Krell was sure of it. In and of itself, a retainer carrying Ga-Vok made equipment was unremarkable. Most were self-equipped and had prior experience in combat. But baring her throat and refusing to show her teeth had been clear signs of recent training in Ga-Vok cultural traditions. Manners of speech could be explained, but body language had to be drilled.

If Gasca knew that opposing Holine was hazardous, and was privately entertaining representatives of foreign powers, then that would also explain why the Seneschal would openly confront Imperial Troops. Gasca was planning for a war with the Empire. They didn't stand a chance against the Imperial Army, but from what he'd seen about Holine's policy decisions, he couldn't blame them for preparing. She wanted her war with Seclora, and no one in their right mind was going to send the next three generations of their children to die for little more than the glory of their Empress. Unless they got most of the Court to side with them, the house of Alicea would die defending their palace.

Krell looked out the window as he sat down in the train. Gasca was beautiful as ever. The station looked up on Mount Heirwat, the sun just settling into the hills behind him. He could see all the colors of the garden, the flowers of a thousand worlds, cultivated beneath thousand-year-old trees that ebbed with magic. Light glittered from the windows of distant galleries and halls, and towers rose high from every corner but one. A single, thin plume of smoke rose from the former home of Atalaine the Enchantress, and Krell remembered his Oath.

"By my breath, my blood, and my bone, I will serve this Empire and all who live therein. If by my death I can preserve its people, I shall do it. If by my life, I can provide for its future, I shall do it." The world turned on raising a hill and shielding the palace from the light of the sun at last. "This I swear, until Death Herself comes for me and relieves me of all oaths."

As the train pulled from the station and the shadows hid the palace from even his lifeless gaze, Krell thought of the other oaths he'd sworn; to have and to hold a wife, now long dead; to protect the father of a woman only recently fallen; and to guide the daughter of a friend, the woman who'd claimed his life.

· · · ·

Although they had experienced regular refinishing and repair, the last major rework of the Empire's shuttleport infrastructure had come in preparation for the Frostbourne War. As such, their design emphasized redundant defensive layers, atmospheric control, and the ability to land and launch large numbers of shuttles in short order. The consensus, when Krell had been privy to governmental decision making, was that the design was satisfactory, if a bit inconvenient for day to day use. In practical terms, visibility on the way in was poor, departures took three times as long as arrivals, and they never felt adequately staffed. It was a system designed for emergencies, not tourism.

Krell knew the general layout well enough that he had managed to cut an hour off of his time by using sally ports and an unused gunnery bunker to bypass most of the outer sections. The third layer assembly area served as the main checkpoint and vendor stalls before arriving at the shuttle docks. He still didn't have the seal though, so he pulled out the tablet, which had been helpfully included with the affects he'd been provided with by the Palace Staff.

I'm at the main checkpoint. Where would you like to rendezvous?

Around him the crowds bustled and hurried. He could smell sausage rolls, all manner of fried food, and the crisp, machine-cleaned air held within the environmental shield. A child was crying in the distance, over by the checkpoint queue a couple embraced their son, and there was a young girl staring into her tablet in line for coffee. Four troopers were clustered near the entrance to the docks, beyond the checkpoint. They appeared preoccupied, but Krell kept them in his peripherals as he began to float among the crowd.

He could easily force his way to the docks. Four troopers wouldn't even be inconvenient, and a crowd like this would guarantee deaths in the panic. There would probably be enough power for him in the chaos for him to teleport anywhere in the Empire. It would be easier than whatever service the_Witch required of him.

The Lich's grasping thoughts were shaken from him as something tugged at his habit. He spun to see what he had caught on and saw a older girl. She was wrapped head to toe in a bandage-like fine silk with only a pair of goggles showing above a matching veil.

"Father, is this your shoe?" she said, playfully dangling a lone shoe from the tip of her finger.

"Who are you?" he replied, scanning his surroundings to see if anyone else was approaching. She raised a single eyebrow while she took a sip from a cream-laden iced latte.

"Why are you even wearing shoes? Are you afraid your feet will get dirty? I wouldn't think that would be a concern for a lich. Or is it just that Neleh give you a really hard time about following the dress code and you're still not completely over it?"

Krell's mind blanked as he put on his shoe. Was this girl sent by the_Witch? She certainly seemed to know a lot about the situation, and she seemed unarmed. If it was a trap, he could probably fight his way out, but if it wasn't, he couldn't afford to walk away.

As he thought, and laced, the girl stepped into an alley behind a single-slice pizza stall and tapped on the door gently.

"My place, if you would?" She listened, then opened the door. Krell could see a poorly decorated apartment, badly lit and smelling faintly of electronics, beyond the doorway. The dimensions of the room didn't line up with the surrounding stall.

"Well?" Krell hastened to catch up, quickly eyeing his surroundings to ensure that they weren't followed. Satisfied in their security, He drifted into the apartment, and was joined by the girl.

"My name is Rea. I'm the_Witch. Don't track any mud around the place."

Small wasn't quite the right way to describe the apartment. Undecorated concrete walls greeted him in every direction, with a series of colorful lights strung along the crown of the room. Besides the bright purple, aqua blue, and soft white lights around the edge of the room, the main source of light came from dozens of screens arranged in a semicircle in what Krell suspected the architects had intended to be a dining room. There was a small two seat table bolted into the floor against the wall across from the entrance. Its scratched laminate surface and single black metal pillar gave the impression that it rightfully belonged in a diner. There was a microwave on the counter, along with a layer of dust over the counters that looked to be several weeks old on the most forgiving of timelines. The trash wasn't overflowing, but appeared to be in better condition than the preserver, which did not appear to be powered. There was a love-seat and a coffee table in the center of the room, facing the collection of screens, albeit from a distance. It was to this last piece that Rea directed him as she crossed the room to a wheeled office chair.

"Just set the wax on the table when you're ready for me to get started on your transit authorization." She spun to face the screens and Krell watched as each screen began to fill with a perpetually updating collection of reports, security feeds, and datasets. He'd been on the command deck of many a warship, and never witnessed as efficient nor as overwhelming an operation as the one unveiled before him in this tiny dump of an apartment. She was doing the work of a high level government official, an arch-administrator to be precise, and she was doing it from what he would guess was a deep urban slum.

"Where are we exactly?" he ventured.

"Porthano, on Castren. They have the most reliable power grid and net access in the Empire, so it made the most sense to relocate here after the war. Not that it wasn't perfectly lovely visiting my home for a few centuries, but it's a lot easier to do my job when the neighbors don't try to chew on my generator. Before that I swapped between a Bureau office on Tuntov and an abandoned broadcast station on Apenii, mostly for the climate, and I worked from home before the quarantine."

"Which war?"

"Frostbourne." she replied, as if it were the most obvious thing in the world.

Krell thought for a moment about what he knew about this girl. The_witch was an alpha+ level admin for the whole net, and no one knew how to contact her or rescind her status. She was a ghost, a legend spoken of in whispers by Net weavers who prayed not to run afoul of her. She was a force for justice that rooted out even small evils and used their own deeds to demand action. She was a menace that left Immortals dead in her wake. It was a bit challenging to reconcile that with the fourteen-year-old and her iced latte.

"I'm not sure I want to ask what quarantine at this point."

"Your loss, I am a verifiable dragon's hoard of knowledge."

"Verified by which dragon?" he scoffed.

"Steffanoricaal, but be sure to call him Steve if you need to pop out for a bit. It'll be much funnier when you do."

She was really hard to read. The screens were non-reflective, and her body language didn't shift for a second. He could hear her typing rapidly even as she spoke, clearing windows as quickly as they appeared.

"My apologies. I'm just finding this all a bit much to take in."

"Really?" She stopped an spun to face him, slowing her chair to a stop with her foot. "Which part? The part where you're a free-willed lich trying to overthrow the Empress of the Nielda, formerly a ranking member of the military and a friend to her father, or the part where I'm older than you?"

"I suppose I might seem a bit nonsensical from the outside."

"Not in the slightest. Everyone I know is special." Rea gestured over her shoulder to point at the screens, then flicked forward, propelling holographic images across the room like a trillion motes of dust. "And I know everyone."

Krell marveled as he watched live footage of farmers, troopers, factory workers, and technicians speed past him. He saw people dying with a name on their lips as those they named watched helpless. He saw tears shed over empty chairs at family tables. He saw a crater in the midst of palace grounds. But, he also saw people gathered around a projection, forming plans. He saw citizens standing tall before their nobles, arguing passionately. He saw a gentle old man, walking with a gardener and carrying a fresh sapling. He saw the Empire, in all its shame and glory. And he saw a girl without parents, a woman who had raised an empire, and an elder who had witnessed history as it was made.

"Oh." he said. And he set the wax on the table.

Chapter Eight
In Which Few Reveal Much

Rea raised a hand and the wax flew through the air before settling on her desk, among a pile of papers and writing implements. She continued responding to reports while Krell stared on in awe at this immortal child.

Then he heard the door knob turn, and the latch click open. He turned to face it, and was lifted off his feet by a glittering silver mist. The Lich screamed in rage, but where it normally would have made an attempt to assert dominance, it instead seemed helpless. In fact, it felt as though the corrupt presence was stretched like a wire frame, and he was merely hanging from it.

"Rea," snarled an unfamiliar woman, "Why is there a Lich in your apartment?"

Rea made no effort to turn. "You remember the man we were talking about the other day? The one the Empress is hunting?" She gave a thumbs up.

The woman appeared in the doorway, and as she fully entered the apartment Krell's vision was interrupted by a being like a cloud. It had the face of an otter, but where the shoulders would have been it simply billowed outward like a mane, filling much of the room and everything he could see beyond it. The otter-lion cloud kept its head facing him as it swirled about the room, but its eyes darted back and forth between Krell, Rea, and the woman.

She was slender, with the posture of a noble and hair whiter than fresh snow. She seemed to glide into the room, her flowing robe only narrowly missing the ground. She was tall, though not quite as tall as he himself was. Everything about her attested to an affinity for ice, but especially the faint fractals featured in her hazel eyes and the white snowflakes that lay patterned across her dark skin. Even now as she scanned over him, he could see a faint sparkling as the colorful lights of the apartment reflected off of her sorcerous features.

"This is some of the most amateurish necromantic spellcraft I have ever seen in this advanced a creation," she said, one hand outstretched. He could feel the magic that held him together being plucked at with every subtle finger twitch the woman made.

"Gee Kate, not everybody has your level of experience," Rea retorted.

"Of course not, but a Lich should be one of the pinnacles of the art. Most of the mages skilled enough to even attempt becoming one have spent decades refining their talents. But how is this one supposed to blend into society..." She twisted her hand and jerked back. Krell felt no pain as his entire right arm fell to the ground, but the Lich was howling as she continued, "...if it can't even use Illusions? And without the second partial-excantation..." She gripped her hand in a fist, leaving only her pinkie extended as she swept the air, causing his ribs to rattle, "...he probably doesn't even know where his iglakosch is."

Krell focused his influence, and forced his voice to work through whatever power she had used to disable him. "I have a pretty good idea of where it is actually."

Kate looked him directly in the eye, a single eyebrow raised. "If you had been crafted properly, there wouldn't even be a question. A proper Lich would be able to treat his iglakosch like a second body, maintaining full and complete awareness of both locations at all times. Why would you be satisfied with this?"

"Kate, this is Admiral Casat. He didn't want to be a Lich."

"Didn't.. want.. to..? Rea, that's nonsense! The things you have to do to become a Lich are unforgivable. Why on earth would you do them if you didn't even want to be a Lich?"

"He didn't do them. Holine did them to him, and then forced the change on him."

"How!" Kate exclaimed disbelievingly.

"I 'unno. You're the wizard." Rea shrugged.

Kate began circling Krell, hand still raised, but now examining him more closely than before. She plucked at invisible strings like a musician, each one causing a part of his body to quiver, collapse, or reset to its normal position. It was painless, but deeply invasive. All the while, the cloud-beast circled, dark eyes never blinking.

"Say," Rea spun to face them, "Why are you here anyway? It's three more days before grocery day."

Kate released all of the strings at once, and Krell settled back to a comfortable hover as his bones began to drift back into place. "I.. may have.. slightly bugged your apartment a number of years ago."

"Junlaerd's fancy hat Kate! Did you even think to ask?"

"I.. no?"

"What made you think I needed you to show up just because I had someone over?"

"I didn't want you to get hurt."

"I'm at the center of almost all knowledge in the Empire. No one was going to sneak up on me!"

"There's a lot of people out there who would want you dead, Rea. I was just taking precautions."

"I know who my enemies are. They're not going to walk through my front door right next to me."

"I'm not worried about your enemies, I'm worried about mine!" The ephemeral otter-lion creature seemed to condense around Kate; its head looking up at her. Krell could see it trailing out from her feet, still laying about the floor of the room, but its focus was now singularly on its mistress as it swatted at the hem of her dress with its paw.

Rea sighed, and released her grip from the arms of her chair. "Okay. Just ask next time you feel a need to carve a whole enchantment into my floorboards."

"Wait," Kate glanced up and met Rea's gaze. "How did you know where it was?"

"Oh, I noticed it years ago, I just didn't bother checking it." She grinned. "What did Petra do to it exactly, I know she made some modifications."

"That troll replaced the mental notification it sends me when she visits with the theme song my mother had written for me back in the day."

"Nice." Rea chuckled, "Always good to hear she still has a sense of humor. Krell, I have your papers ready, we should discuss the service I need done."

· · · ·

"Just to clarify," Krell interjected, "if I don't like your proposal, I can walk away?"

"If you walk out right now, you'll be exactly where you started. You'll have a fuzzy understanding of what was discussed and what you decided, but I'll edit myself out entirely. You know more than I'm comfortable with otherwise." Rea paused, "It won't hurt, and you won't notice."

Krell didn't like the idea of having his memory modified, but he could see why she would be uncomfortable. He knew there was an immortal overseeing all knowledge on the Net, and had been for an unknown length of time. It was a major conspiracy, and he had the power to blow it all up if he talked to the right people, people he knew how to get in touch with no less. Then again, his existence was also a conspiracy, and she hadn't turned him in. She could have, at any moment. In her position, she could have guided the Imperial Guard right to him at any time in the past few days and been completely rid of him. It wouldn't have been of any risk to her either.

"How do I know you're being honest with me?" Krell asked.

"Oh, that's impossible." Rea replied "I've been around longer than almost anyone. No one could prove that I'll do what I say I'll do."

"Why lie when the truth is unbelievable?"

"Because you're a child and sometimes you just want to mess with people," interjected Kate. Her eyes had not turned away from Krell. The creature accompanying her was now moving about the room, a swirling gust of mist snaking back and forth between the two women as it looked after them with its deep colorless eyes.

"I do not!" Rea straightened as she looked to Kate, fingers pressed to her clavicle in dramatic shock.

Kate looked back to Krell. "When you first attempted to find her, you were met by a burst of questionable advertisements, yes?"

He had been, as he recalled, but Kate required no answer.

"It's effective." Rea offered in her defense.

"So is any spam, but they're always dubious 'dating' services or marital aids."

"She sent me weight loss scams actually." Kate shot a Krell a look at his addition, then frowned as she glanced back at Rea.

"Now that is tactless, the man has no weight to lose. In any case, it's childish to be sending people mocking advertisements."

"Now that's tactless. It's not like I'm choosing to be a child; I just am one."

The two locked eyes. Krell shifted uneasily, his habit swaying slightly as he hovered slightly off the ground. A moment passed, and Kate looked away.

"So, Krell." Rea continued, slightly smirking over her recent victory in the contest of wills. "I need you to retrieve a piece of information for me."

"Don't you have access to the whole net? Why would you need me to gather information for you?"

"Holine keeps Imperial Records in a physical archive in the palace. It's been a sore point for the Bureau for years now. It would take decades to push for having them published and there isn't time now. That's my mistake, and I've already set things into motion to prevent it from happening again. As it stands, I only have about a week left and I still need to break into her vault." Rea paused for breath before continuing. "I need you to break into the records, find the location of Holine's hearth, and send me its coordinates and whatever else you can learn about it."

· · · ·

She knew it was a big ask. The alternative was having Kate and Petra help her brute force her way through things, and that would be an enormous problem. Krell had the subtlety and finesse to pull off a mission like this. She just hoped he'd do it.

"What do you mean, you only have a week left?" Rea started considering how much to tell him about her work, "Holine's a Lich?"

"Oh yes, we figured that out years ago. Between her background and interests, budgetary diversions, and ward reworks since her father's passing, it only made sense. I actually suspect that she's helped create at least two other Liches since her own necromorphisis." Krell turned to look at Kate, who was gently petting ZeeGee as she spoke. She glanced about for a moment as Rea also locked her gaze on the pale wizardess. "It's not that impressive, Petra's Mom made eight before she graduated from the Academy."

"She was a prodigy, and her work doesn't pose both a direct threat to our plans and also that is an absolute dork fact to bring up right now," Rea said, but only after a full eye-roll. Kate tilted her head and kept her gaze fixed on the girl in the chair. "And as for your question, Admiral, I have a bit of a calling. I receive the times, means, and locations of death for immortal beings, and it is my responsibility to ensure that they occur. Holine dies on the 15th of the month, in her hearth, of blunt force trauma. And all I know is that the hearth is on Medea."

"So you need me to help you find it, while you break in?"

"Yes. Ideally, you would also kill her so she's there too, but if I can reach her iglakosch with enough time then I can force her to come to me."

Krell leaned back against nothing in particular, his skeletal frame and brown robes being supported purely by the arcane powers that bound his bones together. She could see that he was thinking, and she wanted to give him time to think, but found her feet and fingers starting to vibrate with anxious energy. She needed him to help. She needed him to agree. She needed to not fail again.

Finally he spoke.

"We're going to need more of a plan than this if we're going to break into the palace."

• • • •

"Good Idea. What do you have to work with?"

"I have a ring that causes people who look at me to perceive me as not noteworthy unless I draw their attention somehow, a thorough knowledge of the Imperial Palace, and am a Lich."

Rea and Kate exchanged a glance. Rea turned back to her screens and resumed typing, while Kate stepped toward Krell and extended a hand. "Can I see the ring?"

"Only if you promise I'll get it back."

"Of course. I just want to inspect it. The exact properties of an enchantment can be finicky and I want to make sure there's no tricks or loopholes that might impede its function."

Krell cautiously removed the ring. He turned it over in his hand before placing it in her outstretched hand. Her eyes flashed for a moment as she murmured an incantation and began to turn it and rotate it in her hand. After a minute, she closed her eyes, exhaled, and then handed it back to him.

"It should work well enough to get you into the palace and past outer security, but probably not well enough to get you past any internal checkpoint or inspection. I could probably bolster it if we had time, but it would take a few days. Where did you get it from?"

"A young man on Has-Ket pulled me into an alley while I was being chased by a guard. He threw a cloak over me, handed me the ring, and told me to put it on and stand by the fire with him. Guard ran right past us. I thanked him, he said not to worry, and to keep it." Krell paused, thinking of the gleam in the young man's dark eyes. "He said something about how he wouldn't be able to keep it after his girlfriend caught up with him, and she deserved better anyway. It was sweet, but he seemed like a bit of an idiot honestly, and I needed the help, so I kept it. Checked it over as best as I could too."

Kate glanced over at Rea, who was stifling a laugh. She sighed and addressed the younger woman. "Do you want to tell him?"

"There's so much going on there I don't think that you even know."

"Really? Sounded like one of his worst lies yet to me." Kate looked back toward Krell and pointed at the ring. "Perception filters are a fairly advanced enchantment. It has its drawbacks over invisibility, but it's generally more useful in most scenarios. That narrows down the list of possible enchanters considerably. Based on the runic phrasing I can eliminate everyone taught in the last thousand years, the Khi scroll-loop was eliminated from most perception altering enchantments during the late Pax Gravaga as a redundancy, but the silver filigree isn't showing any signs of tarnish, which means the ring itself has to be relatively new. This limits us to immortals." Kate checked him for a moment for signs of inattention. For his part, Krell was always happy to hear people talk about their passions, and this was clearly one of hers.

"Now, there are only about eight immortals of that age with the skill to craft an enchantment like this. Five of them haven't left Stormgarde since the War, so we can count them out. Cissi and Igor are never seen in public, so they can also be discounted, and Petra stays on the cutting edge of the field so she wouldn't have made a mistake like this quarter back-curl on the top of the Eth."

"That's all eight though?" Krell observd.

"Right! So I had to start thinking outside of mortalkind. Now, this is stylistically incompatible with Elemental enchanting practices, so that only leaves one option. The aura of its diabolic origin is self evident to anyone who knows what they're looking for."

"A Demon?!"

"Yes, but not to worry, see how all of the Phi have an under-loop at the bottom stroke? It's a distinctive flourish seen in the work of Legion. A Demon, yes, but not one prone to curses or underhanded maneuvering. The ring will work as intended and shouldn't come back to bite us later." The otter-lion gave an appreciative purr as it bobbed its head at him from her side.

"A demon made this ring?"

"Yes, do keep up." Kate replied. "Strange that he would take an interest in you. He's usually a bit more petty than that."

"Doesn't seem that strange to me," added Rea. "He probably just wanted a bit of practice and to mess with the authorities."

"Yes, but he doesn't need items to improve his abilities. A perception filter is perfectly within his ability to bestow or use on his own. Why has he been enchanting things lately?"

"Not my place to say." Rea grinned, still holding back laughter.

"If you know what he's up to, you should share it."

"If I thought it was going to hurt anyone, I would. It won't, so it would be rude to gossip."

"If anyone dies because you didn't tell me, it'll be on your head."

"Legion hasn't killed anyone since before you were born, and Petra is fully responsible for that. I see no reason to doubt her ability to keep him from becoming a threat again."

Kate scoffed and the creature chuffed in support. "Fine then." And she turned back to Krell, "So we have you, your ring, Me, and Rea."

"And Petra if needed. School's out for the season and she has the time to spare."

"And Petra," repeated Kate, "just in case. So what's the plan?"

Chapter Nine
In Which A Plan Is Hatched

Krell began to envision the Imperial Palace. The grounds were vast, and held numerous secrets, ranging from concealed artillery and anti-air batteries to the ancient sapient trees that kept silent watch over all of the inhabitants and visitors. Then came The Shell, a kilometer and a half of armored plating that covered the entire palace. Beyond that lay the galleries, the collected art and relics of eight thousand years of the Nieldic Empire. Much of the collection had been created within the palace itself, created by enterprising members of the Imperial family or, often as not, made on commission by request of that same time-tested house. It was, after all, essential to make a name for one's self if one hoped to become the next Emperor.

Now, all of those spaces were easy enough to gain access to. He could most likely just float in with a crowd of tourists or a visiting group of school children. Gaining access to the Imperial Records meant moving beyond the public spaces and entering the palace proper, an entirely more challenging proposition. Entrances were numerous, but none went unobserved.

"You know Rea, It would be fairly simple for me to teleport into the records and collect what you need."

"Sure Kate, but how would we get away with it? Every immortal in the next three galaxies would know you violated the treaty if you went in without the Empress' express summons."

"Maybe if Krell could trick her into summoning ZeeGee here?" This prompted the otter-lion to perk up.

"She'd have to be pretty hard pressed to do that, and I doubt she even knows his name. I mean, the public record identifies that blizzard as being a spell you cast." Rea stopped as if she had finished, but added, "You're welcome for that Zee. It's not your fault mumsie got caught up in all that, is it?" The air got slightly colder as the creature bounced past Krell, the trail of mist extending behind him as he moved over to request skritchings from the younger woman.

"So we'll need a way for a blatantly unliving spellcaster who can only use magic to destroy or create fear to sneak into the most heavily defended location in the known universe."

"I can use a few other spells, but it's particularly draining."

"Such as?" Kate's eyebrows raised as she turned to address the skeleton in the room.

"I've managed planet-level teleportation, and I can perform most conjurings and summons. Still can't manage weapons, but I can conjure small items and magical barriers."

"That could be helpful. Can you conjure anything that would disguise you from a magical ward?"

"I could try to replicate a badge from one of the tour guides. Their quarters are in the private sections of the palace."

"Good!" Rea replied, "let me send you a diagram of one so you can familiarize yourself with it and make it convincing. Will that get you to the records?"

"No, but it should get me into the archives. The physical records are in the under-archive, and are only accessible to an Emperor, their immediate descendants, and designated members of the Bureau. Even I've never been inside."

Rea tapped a few files on her desktop, and Krell's tablet got a notification. "Here's all of the notes I've been able to compile on the defenses of the records themselves. It's taken from cross-talk and commentary by designated bureau members and Imperials over the ages, so I can't promise it's all up to date, but the actual accounts are, obviously, secure within records."

"Of course." Krell nodded. "Otherwise someone might be able to plan a heist." Rea laughed, startling the otter, who dove through his own mist and reappeared behind his mistress, who patted him bemusedly.

"Once you get there, the record you're looking for should be about two hundred years old, probably around the time of the last Emperor's death, give or take a decade. It'll be relatively near the entrance, no more than twenty or thirty meters. Knowing the Bureau, it'll be labeled something like 'Holine, Vault 12, Medea' or whatever. You're looking for the coordinates, and you need to send them to me as soon as you have them. Then you should get to safety as soon as possible."

"Then what?"

"Then Kate, Petra, and I exit this apartment from the door nearest the vault. Kate teleports us to the coordinates. Then we make our way through whatever protections are in place, use her Iglakosch to pull her through if you haven't already killed her, and I end her."

"Do you think that it's likely I'll be fighting her? It sounds like you kind of want me to fight her?"

"Ideally, yes you would. Honestly though, it just seems like it would be really satisfying for you to get in a few last punches before I end her existence permanently."

Krell considered the idea. The Lich, incensed by the knowledge that it had been deliberately hobbled by the Empress, roiled with the idea of destroying its rival. For his part though, Krell could only picture the little girl he used to watch reveling in the stories he told about the exploits and adventures he and her father had protecting the Empire together in their youth. He didn't want to hurt her. He just wanted to be free of this artificial existence.

"We'll see how it goes. I'd rather not if it's all the same to you, but if I must..."

"I'm surprised to hear it," said Rea, as Kate nodded sagely from the plume of softly sparkling cloud. "You're not as bad as the propaganda makes you out to be."

"I should hope not." Krell chuckled.

"Well, then let's get moving, if we don't want to force you into a fight we're going to need all the time we can get!" Kate was reserved, but gestured him toward the door. Krell started toward the door, awkwardly adjusting his clothing so they hung correctly instead of catching on every third rib and bunching on the side of his hip.

"Hang on." Rea spun out of her chair and half-jogged to the door. Even through the light fog that had accumulated in the creature's vicinity, Krell could see her fiddling with her book of fates as she set a hand on the door and began muttering into the door frame. He gave Kate a respectful nod, rose, and began to glide toward the door.

"You'll exit right where we left." She extended a scroll bearing her official seal imprinted upon the wax he'd obtained. "You should be uncontested. I've initiated a few internal affairs investigations to get problem guards removed from duty today, and a lift malfunction on deck four will ensure that they're too understaffed to bother you." Rea stopped for a moment as she took a small satchel off of the mist-hidden counter, or at least he presumed it had been on the counter, and reached in to show him a fresh net-pad.

"I uploaded all of your boarding information here, and I authorized your login to contact me so you don't have to worry about getting sent more ads. It's a much newer model, and I've shielded it so it won't trigger any security algorithms if you take it into a restricted area, take it through a checkpoint, or use it to share copyrighted materials." Rea put the pad back and pulled out a what looked like a necklace of small clay disks.

"These are everkeys. Hold it up to a lock and it will form whatever you'll need in order to unlock it, whether that's a keycard, manual key, a retinal imprint, or a runic phrase etched into a sheet of mica. They don't do particularly advanced arcane locks, or anything with a lot of moving parts, but they'll open nearly anything you're likely to you'll encounter. You can only use them once, so try not to waste them."

Rea reached into the bag again and pulled a cross-shaped piece of metal stored in a carefully fitted leather tube.

"I know what a knife is," chuckled Krell.

"I would hope so! This one also works as a compass, just in case." She returned it to the bag before turning it around. There on the side was the bubbling copper cauldron of the Cauldron Cosmetics Company, carefully embroidered.

"If anything happens, burn the threads on the embroidery and I'll know, even if they have the cameras off."

"I hope it doesn't come to that. I'd hate to destroy your craftsmanship."

Rea blushed and handed him the supplies. He slipped the strap over his head and adjusted his robe so it was a little less obvious that there were no shoulders underneath. Rea took out her book and began to shuffle the pages absentmindedly while he prepared to depart.

"So, I've found out over the years..." Rea started to trail off, and took a deep breath. "Y'know how they always say you only live once?"

"I've heard the saying," Krell replied, tugging at his sleeve to unbunch the fabric caught in his right shoulder.

"It's not actually true. You can live all the lives you want. Thing is, everybody only gets one death."

Krell stopped and turned to face the young woman. She was tightly clutching the book now, and doing her best to meet the flickering blue flames that filled his eye sockets.

"This book has all of the deaths that people have tried to hide and get away from. And... well..." she stopped and tried to gather her thoughts. "You're not in it. I don't see that very much and... Just don't go looking for it, okay? You won't find anything good that way, so just don't."

"Okay?" he replied, falteringly.

"Okay," she stated. And after a moment, she opened the door and pushed him back into the bustling shuttleport, closing the door behind him, and leaving only a janitorial closet in its place.

• • • •

"So, what's the plan for the rest of us?" Kate asked as she scratched the ears of her familiar. Rea turned from the door and removed her helmet and goggles. She began to unwrap her armor and return trinkets to storage while she considered the question.

"We can't do much until Krell gets us the coordinates." she said, as she sat down at her monitor station. It was a relatively true statement. They couldn't move out until he got her the location, but it omitted the range of things she could do in the meantime. She needed to spawn a range of non-trivial sightings around the galaxy to draw the majority of the Imperial Guard out of the palace before Krell arrived, contact Petra to request her assistance, and learn anything she could about both palace security and contemporary Medean trapcraft. It had been a long time since she'd needed to go into the field, and there was no avoiding the steady march of progress, even in magical vault security.

"When should I meet back then?"

"I'll let you know when, and you can just teleport in here."

"Rea, I have plans too. Give me a day to prepare."

"It'll take him two days to arrive at the palace, so meet me back here in three and we'll both wait until we hear from him."

"I'll just cancel my plans then. Will you be contacting Petra or should I?"

"I'll get in touch with her. It's not like she'll take a break for this anyways, so the sooner she knows the better."

"That assumes she doesn't know already." Kate asserted, and without even a blink the universe supported her claim. The towering armored figure loomed behind her, framed by the darkness of the doorway, black sword in hand and a silver gleam on her armor.

"Oh of course I do Kate! I know what you ate for breakfast." There was an audible sound as Petra clapped Kate's shoulder boisterously. The creature reared up defensively, but calmed as it saw the armored warrior.

"Really?" Kate responded, testily rubbing her shoulder.

"Not in the slightest, I just saw that poor friar leaving and thought it was a good time to step in. Good of you to lend him some things, Rea."

"He's going to need it to get me the information I need, doubly so if he wants to get out alive."

"Wait. That was the Lich you were showing me wasn't it? He's got some kind of perception filter, doesn't he?"

"Yeah, a ring he got from a friend of ours actually," Rea answered. As she did, Kate's face lit up and she began to describe, in great detail, the exact artifice of the enchantment. Petra sheathed her sword, doffed her helm, and shot a dubious look at Rea before finally holding up a hand and motioning at Kate.

"Kate, I know how a perception filter works, and I've enchanted enough rings to know how important phrasing is for space conservation. You don't need to tell me."

"Oh." Kate floundered, "I just thought you might appreciate the craftsmanship."

"It sounds pretty good, not gonna lie, but I've never really been much good at visualizing that kind of thing. Maybe you could get him to show me the ring sometime?" Rea stifled a laugh, watching the warrior unconsciously turning on her teaching voice while speaking with the wizardess. Petra handled being magesplained to better than most people with a fraction of her experience, and the softness of her manner would have been disarming to most. Rea could still remember the blood-soaked fields, alight with hellfire, that stretched forth around the deathless knight and her black sword, dripping with the ichor of archdemons. The teacher was a mask she wore; the warrior was her true identity, and no amount of time or nicety would ever convince Rea of the contrary. Even at ease, as she was now, Death's daughter barely moved her hand from the side of her hilt. Rea opened a display at the lowest part of her screens and input a command, bidding one of her trace programs to find Petra's most recent battles. It took only a moment to see the rapidly dissolving body of a Shade, and the terrified, awestruck passers-by who would never know the twisted deeds of the demon lying dead in the streets. Petra was never free, but she was always there to help. Rea smiled and turned.

"I need you to help me enter a Lich's hearth."

Chapter Ten

In Which A Lich Meets An Old Friend And More Art Is Appreciated

It had been a fairly quiet couple days since receiving the_Witch's request. Shuttle trips tended to be fairly quiet, save for the occasional turbulence. The ship he had been booked passage on was moving mostly cargo, so he had only encountered other people while embarking and disembarking at the docks in orbit. His papers checked out, even if there were a few quizzical looks from the trooper that checked them on his way onboard the most recent shuttle, which brought him to the surface of the Nieldic homeworld. Now, as he arrived at the edge of the palace grounds, it had been a few hours since he'd once again felt the ancient magic of the humid planet and its ever-dueling suns.

Before him, barely visible across the vast gardens of the Palace, was the looming rounded shape of The Shell. It would take till the next sunrise to reach it, if one chose to be dramatic, or merely a few hours, if one remembered that the suns rose and set here without intermission. The entrance of the palace grounds were positioned in such a way that the suns would rise from behind The Shell, in order to bring a certain majesty to the experience.

Krell waited for one of the ferries that offered passage through the gardens to stop, then drifted aboard and hovered near the prow. He passed a few coins into the ferryman's hands and held onto the guideline that ran from the bow to the stern of the vessel as it pushed off of the pier.

"First time sir?" asked the ferryman from his platform in the aft. He punted the craft along, expertly guiding the ship through shoulder deep waters.

"No, this was once a second home to me, but that was many years ago." Krell stared out at the rows of neatly trained mangroves and open pools between carefully raised paths. He saw a handful of troopers patrolling here in the outermost parts of the palace grounds. Far from unheard of, but he knew that it meant the Guard were abroad. Walking the gardens was as close to being pulled off of active duty as a member of the Imperial Guard could hope for.

"You with the Guard then?" The Ferryman tipped his wide brimmed hat to a weathered pair of trees that rose above the water like giants, and stretched into the depths like the tendrils of a void drifter. He could see the highest boughs tilt slightly as they passed between them, as if to tip their hats in return.

"Navy."

"Ya' don't say? I served on the *Aristeia* as a Marine. I served on the flight deck mostly, after I lost my leg on Cariol."

Cariol, Krell remembered the battle there with no fondness. One of the last of Arcania's Frost Knights had hidden out there for a few centuries after the end of the Frostbourne War. He'd have kept hiding for a few more centuries if hadn't decided to unleash a plague on the local populace in order to build a new army. Krell had commanded the fleet dispatched to survey the situation, and when a group of marines accompanying an Imperial Guard on a recon mission had sent out a cry for help from 'whoever they send when something kills a Guard', he'd been the only one in range to respond. They'd made him High Admiral for it, and given him a medal, but he never could have done it without the marines who'd rallied to support him.

"Irfield, Ubo, Third Recon. I'm glad to see you made it to retirement. But by the First, you must be two hundred-and-forty and here you are punting a ferry."

"Admiral?" He halted the boat, and it began to spin slowly around his pole. The ferryman pulled off his hat and snapped to attention.

Krell's skeletal jaw shone momentarily as it caught the light of the sunset.

"It's good to see a familiar face."

"Wish that I could say the same sir, where's yours gone off to?"

Krell laughed. It was a hollow, ethereal laugh, but he was pleased to see an old comrade again, even under these circumstances.

"I'm afraid I've lost it. With any luck, I just might catch up with it soon though."

"That'd be a shame sir. If it's gone where I think, I dare say good riddance."

"Really? Was it that bad?"

"If it means losing a man of your caliber, I should think it better for the Empire that we just find you a new one. You know what they say, never lose yourself over a pretty face," and Ubo grinned at his own joke through wrinkles as deep as the waters around them. Krell, for his part, couldn't help but wish to smile along, even if it did nothing to shake his resolve. The best thing he could do was to move on, and ensure that the Empire could move on without him.

· · · ·

" 'Fraid I have to leave you here, sir. Let me know if you need a way out, or a distraction, and I'll do what I can. Best of luck, Admiral." Ubo gave a hearty salute for a man of his age, but punting a ferry around the wetlands like this was probably about as good of exercise as one could hope for. Krell returned the salute, and stepped onto the stone pier that lead up to the path to The Shell. An hour of travel had caused the structure to grow from a menacing shape in the distance to a sky consuming monolith.

A squad of troopers were clustered around a small tower at the center of the ferry station, not so much for security as to be available to respond to threats on the grounds. A pair of skiffs were parked at the nearest pier, with room for a third. Krell knew that each of these towers also concealed a small barracks, mess hall, and recreational area. It was a sub-base to house a full company of troopers and all their equipment. Most of these outposts around The Shell were closed at any given time, along with their respective entrances, but in the event of an invasion, it was necessary to have the facilities in place to house a few battalions of troops.

The navy oversaw none of the surface facilities that protected the Imperial Palace, but Krell had served as the presiding naval officer over the joint operation that updated the standards of living for outposts of this size. It seemed unlikely that Holine, with her desire for an open war with Seclora, had initiated the kind of facility remodels that he and her father, Emperor Kevand, had undertaken a few centuries earlier. She was probably more interested in stockpiling munitions for the Tesserards and increasing the frequency and intensity of Simulated Combat Exercises. Pity really, the men fought better when they liked what they were fighting for.

Krell kept a steady pace as he drifted through the long hall through The Shell. It was, in a time of war, one of the most unpleasant places to be in the known universe. The walls were a perpetual lobster trap of angled walls, designed to provide layer after layer of cover to the defender while forcing attackers into the open. The hall was wide enough for personnel carriers, and tall enough for a fully outfitted war suit, but also forked around fortified weapons platforms every hundred meters. The weapons housed within those bunkers would destroy most armored vehicles, and the troopers at the gun-ports would eliminate any personnel. It was a long way to go, but The Shell had never been breached by an invader since it was first built, supposedly during the Shade Invasion when much of the Empire was overrun by demons. Krell had always questioned this, but since meeting the_Witch he was beginning to wonder what other legends there might be some truth hidden within.

As he passed the final bunker, coming out into the light projected by the illusions that coated the inside of The Shell, he saw a group of children with a handful of chaperons assembling near the door. Most were around Rea's age, by appearance, and had notebooks and pencil cases. Krell drifted in alongside the class and began to follow as a middle-aged man, dressed in the buttoned vest in the traditional Imperial blue, used by most of the palace staff led them into the galleries.

Krell had never received the formal tour of the galleries. He had toured them many times, starting when he was little older than the students he now kept pace with. Most of his walks in the palace had been private, or else accompanied by his wife or some of his aides. His only guided tour had been from Kevand, when they first met in person. He'd been twenty-nine and on leave for the first time in months, so he had taken an invite from a friend he'd met in Realm to go on 'the secret tour of the galleries, the one where you get to hear the stories the guides aren't allowed to tell you'. Had he known as a young Lieutenant that Kevand, the idealist who couldn't handle a sword to save his life (a fact Krell knew only too well after repeatedly saving him from assassins, dragons, and angry bar patrons) was actually the Emperor's grandson, he would probably have been too terrified to go at all. Now, as he passed by the portrait of Hebon the Scarred he couldn't help but wonder if they really did still use that spatula in the kitchens all these millennia later.

"These galleries," droned the guide, "preserve the true history of the Empire, a testament to our longevity and power."

As Krell drew out the tablet Rea had given him and booted it up, he hoped that he really could find that testament here and truly preserve the Empire.

• • • •

There was a full map of his route loaded onto the device, and it even showed the real-time positions of all of the patrolling Guards, cameras, and Krell even saw the Lord of Ufaer lingering at the edge of the displayed area speaking with a pair of guards. It wasn't nearly as impressive as the detailed instructions on the functionality of every lock or the sidebar listing wards affecting the area, but decades of commanding reconnaissance in order to construct battlespace maps did leave him with a certain appreciation for the work that must have gone into assembling this. The fact that it didn't display staff or citizens was unfortunate for tactical purposes, but Rea seemed like the sort of person who didn't want to put them into a tracking system someone else might someday use. He'd have to be careful not to bump into anyone.

The first door was hidden behind an illusion situated between a gallery of bronze castings of the first Nobles of the ten earliest colonies. Hovering above them a series of crystal orbs depicting the star systems that they represented. In the center of the room stood a five-meter-tall marble statue of Captain Hamaf, the commander of the First Ranger Regiment, a unit responsible for securing the crashed ship and guarding the subsequent research project that allowed the Nielda to reach the stars for the first time, which looked out through a window toward the illusory sky. His Great-Grandson had gone on to found what eventually became the Imperial Navy. The actual entrance was an illusory wall behind Queen Collin, the first queen of Tara, who's bust was the last along the inner wall before the room opened up to fit the enormous statue. Krell leaned into the false wall and murmured "The Moon and the Wolves, the Storm and the Sea, In service to Thee," while ensuring that no one was watching him. As soon as he finished speaking, the wall rippled like water and he was pulled into the palace proper.

In direct contrast to the galleries, the inner palace was starkly decorated. While the galleries were a place of beauty, the palace was dedicated to the art of efficiency. The ceilings and halls were less grandiose, their measurements being calculated to ensure that only the largest Nielda risked striking a wall with blade or staff in combat, and not but a few centimeters of leeway given. A single guard could block any hallway in the palace if they so chose, and they had designed every cart accordingly rather than designing the halls to account for Imperial Standards. For what it sought to do, it was without parallel.

Krell hated it. He fully understood why the Imperial Guard resisted all efforts to redesign the palace into a more livable space that the staff could more efficiently work in, but it did not change the fact that they themselves complained incessantly of the challenges of navigating the labyrinthine ziggurat hidden behind a nigh-impenetrable wall and the largest museum in the known universe. He stopped and waited as a guard marched past. The palace had supposedly been redesigned after the Murder of Empress Petra II Wolfhammer by her daughter, Dread Zi-Kah, and her subsequent escape from the grounds; or at least that was the legend the guards used to explain the need for a floor plan that looked like the maze on the back of a cereal box. Krell wasn't even remotely convinced it would have made any difference in stopping her, since it would have slowed down the guard as well, but he was exceedingly confident it would have ensured that he didn't have to look forward to spending the next four hours drifting pointedly toward the cellars to find the Imperial Records located a mere fifteen meters down-east-southeast from the entrance he'd used.

Chapter Eleven
In Which The Witch Packs For A Trip And The Lich Navigates Bureaucracy

Krell was in the palace, but Rea was packing for her trip. She had an old safehouse on Medea they'd be moving to in order to stage their end of the operation. Petra would meet them there, which was a funny way of saying that she had gone ahead to expel whatever gang or creature had moved in, scrub the place down, and then roll in the dirt outside so it looked like she'd walked there from the nearest town. In all the years Rea had known her, Petra had never arrived anywhere clean and that couldn't be a coincidence.

Two bags, one filled with the equipment she'd need to reboot the safehouse uplink until the man in the stupid looking robes got her the location of the vault, and a second with the gear she would need to navigate it. She clasped a box containing two stacks of illuminated cards, each inscribed with a unique magical effect she might need, and set it down at the bottom of a haversack.

She glanced over her jewelry chest. There were dozens of rings, a handful of bracelets in silver and gold, and a score of graven amulets and jeweled pendants. She would want the ring that warned her before she did something that would activate a mechanical trap, a plain gold band with a single blue agate, and the Amulet that prevented wards from identifying her or any of her non-physical qualities, a brass medallion with a featureless face. She scooped up each of them and added them to a smaller pouch. The ring with Rubies and Sapphires that prevented her from being affected by extreme temperatures was usually good to have around, so she added it to the pouch, and decided to bring the pendant with a topaz sandwiched between two pieces of petrified wood, which converted concussive force that would otherwise cause her harm into the sound of a cowbell, as well. She dunked it forcefully into the pouch with a satisfying, hollow clong, and then examined the bracelets. There was a platinum braid, which she could use to shoot a dart into most surfaces within fifty feet, and then support up to three hundred kilograms of weight without dislodging unless desired, or she could take the set of eight golden bangles that would multiply her physical strength by ten and make her grip strong enough to break stone. It was a tough choice, on the one hand swinging across chasms was super fun, on the other hand, the bangles would look better against the gray of her outfit than the braid would. Theoretically, she didn't need to choose now, but she still had to fit the rest of her outfit into the bag and she was running out of time before Kate arrived. She grabbed the bangles and cinched the pouch shut over them.

Her armor and wraps were added to the haversack, along with her cap and a large collection of talismans she kept with them, although she tucked the one that kept her from being tracked by cameras into her pocket alongside her personal tablet, and the one that made her surroundings look like a beach to unwelcome scrying attempts in the other. Then she began to pull at the drawstrings in an effort to close the over-packed bag.

There was a faint pop beyond the door, and ZeeGee swooped across the room, twirling around her excitedly as Kate entered the room.

"Rea, are you?.." Kate looked at the sloppy haversack, then twirled her hand and a burst of wind lifted it into the air. The drawstrings drew taut, and the bag set down again properly fastened. Kate wore a half-grin as she continued. "Are you ready to go?"

"Show off. Yeah, I'm ready."

Kate stretched out her hands, "Then come, and let's be off." Rea pulled the pack onto her back and shouldered the haversack. A cold wind swept past her as ZeeGee enveloped his mistress' right arm, his face pushing out of her hair over the opposite shoulder. Rea took her left hand and nodded. The door shut itself as the trio vanished.

· · · ·

Krell quietly slid into the Records Lobby, narrowly avoiding the vision of a passing guard. The sign over the desk was hyper legible, white with black outline on a light brown background using the designated lettering of official Bureau of Records and History signage. The room's only other occupant was a woman in her mid second-century with the distinctive shoulder patch of the Eye and Tome, very clearly an administrator with the Bureau.

"Please input your identification information and take a seat. Someone will be with you shortly, just as soon as they have finished helping prior citizens. Thank you for your patience," came the overhead voice, ever chipper and mildly off-putting. The woman at the counter gestured toward a keypad and screen near the entrance without looking up from her book.

"You can skip the sitting part. I'm available when you're ready."

Krell paused as he considered entering a false identity. Anywhere but the bureau and he wouldn't have even considered it, but the raw apathy that the entire organization gave off was both mind-numbing and also aggressively neutral. Short of an existing request for his detention, the bureau wouldn't bother him, and they'd slow down Holine herself if she came looking for him while she filled out whatever forms they needed in order to pursue him. Probably a J80x-Intradiction of fugitive within a Bureau managed facility or something, they all followed a strict naming convention. He leaned into the keypad and typed, hoping there wasn't a standing order on his account. The screen flashed a number, 01-001, and the words 'please take a seat and wait for your number to be called.' But Krell followed the administrator's instructions and proceeded to the counter past ten rows of identical, dusty chairs. He halted a foot from the counter, and even several inches above the ground, he looked up at the woman who would decide how difficult it was going to be to get into the Archive.

"Casat, Krell, age 383, Rank at time of separation, Grand Admiral, Current legal status: Deceased. Do I have all of that correct?" The woman had yet to look beyond her counter, staring at a screen filled with every detail of his life.

"That's correct."

"Mister Casat, I don't have a current address for you. Would you like to update that at this time?"

"I'm afraid my current occupation doesn't provide for a stable living situation."

"I'll just put you down as transient then." She tapped on a few buttons before turning to face him. There was a flash of concern as she locked eyes with the steady flames that lingered in his hollow sockets, but it was replaced with speed, professionalism, and efficiency as she continued, "Now then, what can I do for you?"

"I need to find the location of a vault on Medea. It would have been constructed early in the reign of Holine the Fourth, by her direction or the direction of one of her subordinates to contain an iglakosch."

"I'm afraid you're not authorized to enter the Archives. If you need a general inquiry, I can pull up your authorizations and assign a member of Bureau staff to retrieve information on the subject in three to five days."

That wasn't nearly fast enough, Rea only had about two days before Holine's death was foretold, and the consequences seemed vague, but her worry had been very real.

"Can I open a specific inquiry?"

"Do you have keywords?"

"Holine the Fourth, Medea, and Hearth. Only including results containing all keywords."

"Cydrek!" she shouted, and Krell watched a loose pen on the counter bounce twice before rolling off the counter into the hands of a looming humanoid form. "Cydrek, Level 2 authorization, locate files containing all of the following keywords: Holine the Fourth, including all variant depictions, Medea, and Hearth. Return with all relevant documents you can find, return within the hour."

Rather than moving, the rough hewn stone servant raised a hand, "Query." Boomed a harsh masculine voice. "Was this request made by the entity Krell Casat?"

"Yes."

"Reply. Level One Authorization exemption order active. The Entity is to await here. A secure box addressed to The Entity has been placed here to await his arrival. This Unit must deliver The Entity his secure box before complying with the Administrator's inquiry. Regrets are to be offered. By order of Dowager Empress, Vice Admiral Neleh, I am sorry for the inconvenience, Administrator." And as the Administrator began to splutter in confusion, Cydrek's booming strides carried him back into the depths of the Under-Archive.

The box was fairly small. Cydrek had carried it delicately between his arm-sized fingers but even on a table in front of Krell, it was a little smaller than a tablet. He entered his key-code and opened it carefully. He and Kevand's wife had gotten along rather well in her time as his second-in-command, but the seal on the box marked it as having been entered some thirty years after his death. There was no way to be sure she hadn't changed her outlook in the intervening decades.

Inside was a letter and a shallow rectangular jewelry box. Krell took the letter carefully, and began to read it aloud under Cydrek's vigilant, yet curious, watch.

Old Friend, I am so sorry.

I hope you find this before too long. I am old, and cannot wait much longer. Without the aid of foul and evil magic, I will pass on all too soon and join our Kevand. Given your condition, I know that you can relate to my plight. Regrets must be set aside, but know that you are well-missed.

Penalupa and I sought the truth for many years after your passing. The circumstances of your death were of great concern to us, as your passing was sudden and unexpected, much as my husband's passing was. Alas! We found what we sought, and would that we had known sooner that we might have prevented your fate.

Still, we delved further into the secrets my daughter has foisted upon the Empire. We found record of a vault on Medea, but her agent, a Lich posing as her own guard, was able to destroy it before we could expose her as a Lich herself. We have hidden its coordinates on the back of this letter, in the hopes that you may one day destroy it. Better still, we discovered that this very same Lich carries your iglakosch. If you can find him, and destroy him, perhaps you can finally be free from this wretched fate brought on by my traitor daughter, who has usurped my husband's throne and seated herself by falsehood and treachery.

Krell couldn't bear to read the signature as the significance of Neleh's words began to settle into his heart. Immortality was disqualifying for a member of Nieldic Nobility, though not truly criminal. But usurpation of the throne implied one of two things, and Krell remembered the coronation. It had not come by threat of force. That could only mean one thing; Holine had murdered her own father for the throne.

Suddenly the letter burst into flames, and Krell spun around to see an Imperial Guard wearing the triple braids of a captain and the markings of the 1st guard division on his chest standing in the doorway. He ignored the keypad to the side as the voice of the Bureau asked him to take a seat. The Administrator stood behind her desk and pointed harshly toward the keypad.

"Take a number, Captain." She spat. "If you're here to arrest the Admiral, you need to fill out a J80x Intradiction of a known fugitive within a Bureau managed facility form. No exceptions." No sooner had she finished speaking than she was hurled backward into her office by a frozen spear. The guard chuckled as he drew his staff.

"Hello Krell, It's time for you to come back to work." He slammed his staff against the tiled floor.

Krell watched a necklace clatter against his armored chest. Even from across the room, he knew the words etched on the back of the locket that matched the one hanging from his own neck, 'May the Empire and His Majesty ever prosper -N&K', and the pictures within: the joyful bride in her dress uniform, the last day she had cause to wear it before Krell himself had issued her order of dismissal, and a young admiral, with his neatly trimmed beard, serving his favorite posting as Best Man to the future Emperor. As Kevand's necklace hung from the neck of this traitor captain, Krell felt fury, and an icy grip pulled him from command as the Lich took sight of its iglakosch.

Chapter Twelve
In Which The Witch Gets Dressed Up

Cydrek rushed from behind the Lich and crashed through a nearby wall, cradling the impaled and furiously shouting administrator all the while as he carried her to safety.

"Or, you could put up a little fight, make it fun for us both? Nothing stopping me from going all out, We both know you'll just be back in front of me soon enough." The captain tapped the necklace with the tip of his staff.

The Lich required no encouragement to engage. As Kate had pointed out only a few days earlier, it was made for destruction alone and with its only vulnerability in front of it there wasn't even a question of what needed to be done. Take the iglakosch, no matter how many deaths it took.

A roar filled the room as flame began to fill the space, torrents of bright orange washed over Holine's Captain. He began to laugh and swept the air before him, deflecting the worst of the blast into the nearby walls. Daggers of black ice formed in the air as he clenched his fist, then hurtled forward as he jabbed in Krell's direction.

Krell watched helplessly from within his own skeletal form as the last scraps of the letter burned away. With it went the last record of Holine's Hearth and all hope of stopping her. A few more moments and he could have teleported the letter to Rea and her friends, or at least seen the coordinates himself and let his memory serve as a record of that knowledge. Now it was too late; There was no way to find the information Rea needed and stop whatever threat Rea's journal helped her to forestall.

He hoped she wasn't watching this. The girl was clearly burdened by so much already without also having her plans ruined by his own failure. He hoped she wouldn't watch him be overpowered by this sadistic brute, alone and stripped of control by his own twisted impulses. This belligerent engine of destruction was going to be feinted into its own demise. It didn't even have a proper connection to its own iglakosch.

The Lich took a grueling hit from a pillar of ice that trapped its foot to the ground and frantically began to melt the pillar enough to free itself as Krell continued his thoughts. Kate had said that an iglakosch should serve as a second body, from which a Lich had full awareness of its location and surroundings. He lacked that sense, but he doubted Holine would eliminate such a useful benefit entirely. Most likely, she would have altered the enchantment instead, causing it to send that input to her. As frustrating as the implication that she was watching his pathetic efforts to fight her captain was, it did mean the iglakosch was connected to her. And that meant that someone adequately talented at reading ley lines and enchantments might be able to trace the connection and maybe even use those patterns to trace her connection to her own iglakosch. If there was anyone he knew who could do that, it would be Kate. It was a risk, but he needed to get to that iglakosch and send it to her.

As the thought crossed his mind, he felt a resonance. All that the Lich wanted was to keep the iglakosch out of the hands of its enemies, and all Krell needed right now was to send the iglakosch into the hands of his allies. For once, in all their centuries together, they found themselves in accord.

Krell watched, pointing out the idiosyncrasies of their foe: the way he moved, how the air began to shift as he cast his spells, and where the gaps in his armor showed. The Lich began to gain the upper-hand, countering attacks and delivering more precise and effective blows. Quickly the balance of their duel leveled, and then tipped in their favor as icy bolts dissipated in the burning air and waves of orange flame turned to blue-white tongues of destruction that carved into their foe. Finally, as the captain tottered back as the air combusted before his face. Krell and the Lich reached out, grabbed the necklace, and pulled it free. The two pooled their strength, picturing Kate and her misty companion as they cast their iglakosch across space, hoping that it would find refuge with her.

All at once Krell felt the drain of the spell. It was unwise to teleport to an unknown location, as all mages knew, but unable to die he felt his awareness fade; the Lich clattering feebly to the ground as they spent every drop of their power on that one desperate spell.

• • • •

Rea was browsing the latest report. A private meeting between Gasca's Seneschal and representatives of the five strongest Ga-Vok clans was being attended virtually by representatives of 89 other ruling Nieldic noble houses, and six of those not attending virtually had arrived for a 'trade summit' earlier that morning. Based on Krell's observations, this was likely part of a move toward revolt in the event that Holine had the Nobles themselves executed. Given that the report prior to this showed that a wing of the mage ward of the Imperial Palace Prison had just replaced routine staff cleanings in favor of confidential security assignments by members of the Guard, she was inclined to believe that they were making the right move. The_Witch issued a blanket override for Holine's required notification of any inter-noble conferences; Rea saw no reason why such a clearly mundane meeting needed to be brought to the Empress's attention.

There was a small pop, and Rea opened her rear-facing view. ZeeGee spiraled through the room, and placed a newly appeared necklace into Kate's hand. Beyond the haunches seated firmly in her own lap, she could feel a wagging in the direction of what qualified as the familiar's tail. He'd found an exciting new thing for mom.

"What's up?"

Kate turned the necklace in her hand for a moment, taking in the basic details. Her brow furrowed as she inspected one side of the small pendant, and then she clicked a button at the top. "It appears to be a locket by construction," Her eyes flashed and the locket flew upward in a steep arc as the wizardess shot back into her seat. It was caught midair by ever-attentive ZeeGee, who deposited the now rime-coated jewelry into Kate's hand as she recovered. "And heavily enchanted. My apologies; it doesn't look the part."

"Probably wasn't meant to be enchanted. How'd it get here?" Rea asked as she watched a series of feeds be cut within the Imperial Palace for 'routine maintenance'. A clear lie, as she had never been consulted, let alone seen a request for authorization, in regards to performing any sort of maintenance. The necklace lifted into the air between Kate's hands as she began to enunciate incantations. Threads of shadow, royal purple, sickly green, and a single sky blue thread, began to appear in the air around it.

Rea zoomed into the locket as she began recognizing the nature of the magic. There was a picture of a woman in a wedding gown, dagger at her side and with a smile like an old chess-master. Across from it was a young man in full dress uniform, sword at his side, and a grin like a boy on an adventure with his paksneif. As the necklace slowly spun, Rea read the engraving on the back 'May the Empire and his Majesty ever prosper -N&K'.

"It appears to be someone's iglakosch, but I can't say I recognize..."

"It's Krell's iglakosch." Rea interjected. "The necklace belonged to Emperor Kevand the Fourth. It was a wedding present from his wife and best man." An anger took root in her as young Krell's smiling face spun by again. This was how he lived, happy to serve his friends. He'd given his life to the Empire, his heart to its people, and that ungrateful, usurping, WARLOCK had stolen it from him!

"The blue one will be him. What about the others?" she asked through clenched teeth. Kate looked over in surprise.

"Uh..Oh, Okay." Kate plucked carefully at the other threads for a moment, tilting her head slightly as she considered their motion.

"These ones." she motioned at the threads of darkness, "are drawn from the fear of those around him. Triangulating them with the blue string, I'd say he's still in the Imperial Palace. These ones," and now she gestured at the handful of sickly green threads, "are dud threads Holine didn't know how to make the iglakosch without, but should enhance his magical abilities and allow him to do most of what you and I would expect from a Lich. If it were me, I would have tied them off so they couldn't be traced, but luckily she's tied all of them to," and now she gathered the purple threads in her hand, "herself. These are the threads that should have given him the ability to perceive the iglakosch and freely move it as he pleased."

Rea started up, but found herself unable to do so with ZeeGee's near infinite presence in her lap.

"Don't worry, I blocked that as soon as I realized what this was. I've actually," Kate plucked one of the threads playfully, "removed her entire memory of arriving here. As far as she knows, this necklace exists in an athermal void right now, and has since it left the palace." Rea settled back into her deeply cold, yet comfortable seat. "It's really quite lucky that she tied so many of these things to herself. For us at least. I should be able to find her iglakosch in the time it takes for you to get dressed with all this evidence."

• • • •

Rea pressed the bonds together on her armor padding. Ten thousand years of progress had culminated in a soft, thin quilt of fabric, sewn to conceal interlocking pouches of kinetic gel. It served to absorb concussive force and greatly lessened kinetic energy from blaster fire. It wouldn't stop everything, but it would keep her on her feet. The loose fibers on the seams knit each other together to form an unbroken under-layer for her armor.

Then Rea began to strap on her armor. She started with her greaves. Petra had crafted them by pressing layers of stiff leather together around a layer of horn belonging to the dragon Kierarsubal, onto which she had traced, in fine lettering, a poem describing a cat twisting itself in the air before landing on the pinnacle of a bell tower. Their grace would allow her to land softly from any height, and always on her feet. Then, she pulled on her bracers, an ancient sigil carved on their outer length mirroring Kate's beloved Standing Stones. Neither wizard's spell nor naval shell, or any force of man or hell could break the barrier formed by their divine ward, so long as she held her hands aloft. She tightened the straps until she felt the gel beneath stiffen and hold them in place.

At last, she lifted her breastplate over her head, and lowered it onto her shoulders. Petra had not crafted this piece, for Rea had owned it since before the paladin had first raised her smithy's hammer. It was covered in images of ruin and flame; shattered swords and shivered bolts formed the margins of a depiction of battle. A woman with an axe in each hand, and legs like a wolf howled from her left. Her triumph was matched by a proud Ga-Vok warrior on the right, his head high in humility and his hands resting upon the guard of a sword two feet his better. Beneath them lay a great demon, the second Rea had slain, whose name she had smote from the world. Alicea and the Alpha had worked together to make this armor for her, when her experience had been only a little beyond her years. The Demon's Hide was impenetrable to all but a select few enchantments and spells, and moved with her like it were her own skin. She could feel her mythic companion's love as she saw their joy looking back at her from her mirror.

For those parts of her that remained uncovered, and to conceal her identity from anyone she might encounter, Rea wrapped herself in yards of grey steel-silk. A fool wizard had once thought to craft armor of spider's silk, and spent centuries breeding and experimenting with spiders so that they could be milked for silk enough to form suits of armor. He had died a failure, but his apprentice had seen the work to its true conclusion, as he managed to create a new species of spider that spun an iron silk which could be harvested without killing the spider. Although costly, there were few ways of making armor more resistant to blades, without the aid of Dwarves and their star-silver, and none more flexible.

As she wrapped herself, Rea slowly added talismans. A charm to protect from wards against sight and a token to remain unseen from those born under too few moons found their homes besides a figurine that could be set upon the ground to create an automaton that would open any door and a little blackbird that could remember and repeat anything said in the voice of a child. She wore a half dozen rings, and the chains of necklaces bunched beneath the silk as she moved.

Lastly, Rea pulled on her cap. Its leather was unhardened, meant for padding rather than deflection, and it came with a pair of goggles enchanted to show the unseen things around her. She could see the way ZeeGee and Kate's shadows merged in the deep mist he exuded, and the rings and threads the wizardess had formed around the ones that ran skyward from Krell's iglakosch. She could see the small dark box around the small flitting eye at the end of the purple threads. She reached under her desk and pulled her last two belongings out.

The notebook she slipped into a pouch on her hip, where it wouldn't fall into the wrong hands. The other she toyed with, turning it in her hands as she looked at Holine's curious eye in its illusory surroundings. It was her Father's knife, a handle of Nieldic bonesteel with a blade of pure red crystal, formed by a spell already ancient by the day of her birth. Most Nielda considered Bloodstone to be a secret kept only by the Imperial Guard, but there was a time when many had known its use. There were few enchantments it couldn't pierce, and few more that would resist it.

"Do you know where we're going?" Kate looked up and several of the threads twanged slightly as the divinations faded.

"About forty miles east of here, under the mountain. The vault is guarded, but nothing we can't handle."

Rea nodded, and took the necklace in her hand. "Drop the illusion?"

"Alright." The box faded and Rea found herself eye to eye with the Empress.

"If Death Herself hasn't let you know yet, be sure to say hi for me when she comes for you." The blade glinted in the light and the eye vanished as the associated thread fell slack. Space contorted and the necklace vanished as it was pulled across the void.

Rea held out a hand to help Kate up, and she grinned. "Let's go kill the Empress!"

Chapter Thirteen
In Which Someone Is Summoned Away

Kate's teleportation spells were a marvel to experience, easily Rea's favorite way to lose a meal. It was like holding onto a snowflake; cold, challenging, and left you with a distinct curiosity about why you had tried such a thing in the first place. The accompanying array of sensations were just as unique as the places to which you might be bodily dragged across the void toward, but with none of the amenities of conventional travel. And so, readjusting her wrappings to cover her mouth, and kicking some of the local flora over the former contents of her stomach, Rea stood and began to trudge after her unfaltering travel companion, toward the sound of blaster fire.

A spray of purple-white energy fused a part of the dune to their side into a twisted piece of glass as the entrance to the vault came into view. An armored warrior had dispatched a drake and several automatons. A heavy turret, suspended above the entrance, was beginning to glow as its levitative field strained against the single hand that aimed it toward the ground as the warrior waved cheerfully toward them.

"Hello Rea, I see teleportation still doesn't agree with you. Do you need a fizzy water? Or maybe some physician's chalk?"

"I've had worse," Rea replied. "At least this time I didn't end up at some backwater tourist trap."

"I'm hurt." Petra replied, her armor clinking as she dramatically clapped a hand to her breast. "I thought you liked our little trip."

ZeeGee did a quick circuit around Petra, before staring disdainfully at the sun and retreating to the comfort of Kate's shadow. The Wizardess had advanced to the door beneath the turret, which was beginning to overheat as it continued attempting to direct its aim toward any of the three women. She brushed the dust from the fortified entrance, thought for a moment, and then made a small gesture with her ring finger. There was a loud, twisting, crunch before the door fell ajar, with one side at a sharp 45 degree angle and the other slumped into its track, scraps of the locking mechanism dangling within its half-meter thickness.

"We're in. Petra, would you care to take point?"

"Sure!" she replied, her black sword dislodging itself from the drake and flying into her hand. She passed the tip of the blade under the turret's mount and Rea watched the enchantments shift as Petra rewrote them. When she released the turret, it powered down its weapon, and began to hum a simple, happy tune.

The three began to proceed further into the vault. Rea pointed out which parts of the floor would trigger poisoned darts, what parts of the ceiling would slam downward to crush intruders, and where the dust was disturbed by protective golems. And as she did, Kate would dismiss protective wards and dismantle glyphs that would curse thieves, Petra cut through guardian automatons and bound undead, while ZeeGee bounced along about them.

After opening a particularly imposing door, they found themselves under a tremendous dome. In the center of the room there was a statue of volcanic glass, a turtle, with crystalline spikes emerging from its shell, with the face of a jackal. The elemental roared as the three women readied themselves for battle. Before Petra could leap forward, her hand already on the grip of her sword, Kate held up a hand to stop her, and the room filled with mist. A piercing echo of the elemental's roar reverberated through the entirety of the chamber, and they found themselves unable to budge until the mists receded. Kate lowered the hand to scratch the small bluish otter-lion's head. Rea smiled in satisfaction as Petra relaxed her grip on her sword, and stepped over a set of gargantuan, thawing chains.

"Ah, right," Petra commented.

"Y'know, I thought it was weird that we hadn't run into any bound elementals in here yet. They're normally such a staple of good dungeon design," Rea added.

"Really? I'd never waste one on a dungeon," Kate concluded, smiling as ZeeGee bounded cheerfully beside her.

It was after the fourth non-regulation compliant walkway over a chasm of apparent doom that Kate stopped dead in her tracks and Rea watched ZeeGee's ear twitch. His eyes widened as he looked to Kate and then, with a bark of protest, he was pulled from sight by an unseen force.

Kate's hand was halfway to her familiar when he vanished. Her eyes glazed over as her mind left the vault. She spread her hands wide in the air, feeling at the threads of magic in search of one in particular. Her body seized as she took hold of a pale blue thread, woven together with one of a gleaming grey. She tugged at it, first gently, then more frantically. Rea watched in surprise as Kate spun a glowing ring from loose threads nearby and cast it up the thread and beyond the rocky ceiling of the tunnel. She watched after it, her brow furrowing and expression growing more dour.

"I'm going to go deal with something," she said through gritted teeth, meeting Rea's gaze. "Don't wait for me."

And she snapped her fingers, and vanished herself.

Chapter Fourteen
In Which His Highness Begins To Weep

Rea looked at Petra. "She just left."

Petra pushed the latest automaton from her blade as a blast deflected off of her armor. "Sounded serious. Someone must have summoned Zee, and that can't be good." She threw her sword at the offending turret, skewering it with the shadowy blade before catching it by the returning hilt. " I'm sure she'll be fine though. Kate's very good at what she does."

"Yes, but what about us?"

"Oh, we'll be fine too. You've got more experience than anyone with this sort of thing and we're easily halfway there."

Rea's thoughts turned to Krell, languishing somewhere in the palace. "Do you think that maybe Kate will take the opportunity to break Krell out while she's away?"

"Wouldn't put it past her." Petra caught a false stalactite in her free hand as they both heard a click from the floor. "She can be very kind when she lets herself, and he certainly doesn't deserve to be locked up."

"No, he really doesn't."

"It'll be okay, Rea. We've got this!"

After Rea and Petra had passed over another doom chasm and a room with a statue that fired lasers from its eye, Petra leaned against a door, while Rea was carefully picking its lock.

"So, did you talk to anyone yet?" Petra asked.

Rea stopped after disarming the alarm, remembering their earlier conversation. "Yes, actually."

"Well?"

"His name is Krell, and his favorite color is grey, like a Taran fog." Petra hit her in the shoulder, causing a tumbler to jam in place. It was playful, but even a playful punch from the Demon slayer was a little painful. Rea started to pry the tumbler loose so she could finish opening the lock as Petra continued. "That's a security question! Tell me something about him he had to tell you himself."

Rea thought back to all of their interactions. They'd never really talked about him, or what he liked and wanted. As she thought, she turned and prodded at the lock, but much like her memories, she couldn't find the solution within it. Then it clicked, the door swung open, causing Petra to stumble into the next hallway.

"Petra, am I a bad friend?"

Petra regained her footing and looked back at the young woman. "Yeah, you kind of are," she replied, after a moment's hesitation.

"Oh." Rea shoved her tools back into a secure fold in her wraps, "then why are you doing this for me?"

"Even if you're kind of rude, I know you're doing your best to keep other people safe. You might not be a good friend, but you pulled me out from under that cruiser back in the Shade Invasion, when even I didn't want to get out." Petra sighed. "You're kind of a bad friend, but I know you could be a really good one if you tried."

And the two immortals silently decided that the doorway was a perfectly reasonable place to rest for a moment, as Rea broke down.

• • • •

Krell awoke in a cell. He couldn't tell which of the Imperial Palace's three cell wings he was in, because they were designed that way, but he could feel the deep concern emanating from the cells around him, and even outright fear from the cell across from him. It seemed like a severe mistake on Holine's part to have put him in an occupied wing, but he was grateful for the second chance it would grant him.

The wall with the door was polarized, with the opaque side facing him, but he could feel the fear from across the hallway in the next cell. Krell rose off his feet and drifted to the wall, hoping to get a glance at his fellow prisoner. Holine must have been skipping out on the maintenance budget because, as he pressed against the wall, there was a flicker as the magic sustaining him began to interfere with the static field that kept the wall polarized.

Across the hallway was an old man, probably into his second century. His hair was white, and his skin was loose over muscles no longer as well defined as they had likely been in his youth, though not so loose as to completely hide those that remained. He wore a fine embroidered vest, a little dirty from mishandling, with a silver broach of a wolf.

"Your Highness? King Athalion the Third?" The figure stirred as Krell's sepulchral voice carried across the room. He looked frightened, then pressed himself against the wall and looked frantically about before meeting Krell's gaze.

"You're the Lich, the one Holine is hunting. Or was hunting I suppose, as we are now both her prisoners. I am he, I am Athalion, King of Gasca."

"And I am Krell Casat, formerly of His Majesty's Navy. I'm sorry that we must meet again like this. Your mother introduced us when you were younger." Krell chuckled a low, haunting chuckle. "I'm afraid I finally do look my age though."

Athalion smirked as he recalled his own comments on first meeting the late Admiral, and he relaxed a little. "Then we are in the same boat, for I carry my years also. It's good to see someone with more bones to pick than I in this forsaken place."

"I wish that were truly so, but I'm afraid my bones are picked nearly clean now, and I bring fresh fuel for your fire."

"Oh?"

Krell hesitated. The pain he was going to cause this kindly old man would be enough to shatter the prison bars with enough to spare for the battle ahead, but for that very same reason, he did not wish to deliver the news.

"Your Granddaughter is meeting with representatives from the Ga-Vok about the situation. I have no doubt she is not alone."

Athalion nodded. "She's a cut from Alicea's own dress, I would expect nothing less from her."

"She's ejected a contingent of Imperial Troopers from the planet."

"As is her right as Seneschal. You're avoiding something. Don't spare my mind over your fears; I am ready."

"From my own experience, no man is ready. If you insist though," Krell wavered, then he drew back from the wall so he could not watch as he spoke, "Your daughter Atalaine is dead."y

There was a silence that penetrated so deep into the room that Krell could hear the machinations of the Lich stop as the grief began to flow into him. The little bones of his hand began to shake as the power flowed into him, and he rose into the air involuntarily as fears culminated and pain swelled. As the power of the Lich began to swell, Krell directed that power into the door, causing it to flicker and then shudder and collapse in a heap of crushed scrap.

"How did it happen?"

"I came to her seeking wax for a seal so I could come here. A guard saw me and we fought. There was an explosion and she was crushed by the rubble. She wanted me to save you."

With the wall now rolling back on itself in his aura, Krell could see the tears that caught in Athalion's well kept mustache and neatly trimmed beard as they rolled from his eyes.

"I'm sorry your Highness. In this form, I could not wield the spells that would have let me save her. I.."

"Go." The king of Gasca lay slumped in the corner of his cell, "go and leave me to grieve my daughter, harbinger."

Krell began to drift toward the end of the cell block, where a handful of troopers were beginning to assemble, but stopped. He gestured to the other cell doors, turning their locks to ash with a deliberate thought. As they swung open, he knelt before the king. He reached up to his own neck, removed the necklace that hung within his chest, and lay it down beside the weeping father. Then he took the ring from his finger, and set it beside him.

"This ring will allow you to hide yourself and sorrows from any you do not wish to speak with. I hope the locket will remind you that you need not face them alone."

Krell left the man, and turned to face what he hoped would be his final battle.

Chapter Fifteen
In Which An Otter Is Most Distraught

The door to the throne room opened. At the far end of the room were fourteen individuals, with a few more scattered throughout the hall. The handful of junior guards quickly formed a loose defensive line between Krell and the throne as he rose into the air, white flame dancing across his outstretched arms. Twelve of the thirteen captains assembled at the foot of the dais exchanged quiet glances, while the First Captain began to walk briskly toward him.

"Lich. You dare enter the Imperial Throne Room!"

"Jomran, did you know how she came to the throne or are you just a fool?" Krell hovered, drawing power from the quaking junior guards as he began to gauge the other captains. Jomran should have commanded the thirteenth by now, and the weathered, bent husk of Ilkar, Kevand's former Captain, must have been a constant reminder of that fact. The other eleven were no fools, and each a master mage in their own right, no doubt there was some suspicion by now that something was awry.

"I am well aware, Lich. I stood by her side through the coronation, and testified to her beneficence before both councils."

Krell shuddered, flames surging around him. The robes began to burn away as he stared at the traitor before him. "As High Admiral of His late Majesty's Imperial Navy, you stand accused of High Treason against the Empire, Aiding and Abetting a Traitor, Accessory to the Murder of an Officer of the Imperial Navy, and Accessory to Usurpation. Who will answer this accusation?"

The captains straightened, save withered Ilkar. The aging captain of the thirteenth raised his staff and clapped it against the palace floor. His voice was a shadow of its former self, "Krell? Is that you?"

"It is, old friend. I stand as witness to the crimes, and offer my memories as testimony." Krell remained a meter aloft, only two columns into a room that stood twenty-five deep, watching a handful of the more tactical guards lurking past the second row, which stood beyond those pillars flanking the central passageway. There were no true windows in the hall, but the room was lit by the days and nights of the hundred palaces shown in the screens along the walls.

"Enough!" boomed the voice of the woman on the throne at the far end of the hall. Holine rose from the throne, descending a single step of the hundred steps that rose up the dais holding the seat of Imperial authority. She gestured harshly as she raised her hand. "You will not sully this court with your presence any longer. Seize him."

"He was your father!" Krell cried, a tongue of flame rolling from his eye sockets as the fires within them flared. "He loved you; we all loved you!"

"I command you to seize him!"

But the captains did not move. Ilkar shook his head, the crest atop his helm exaggerating the motion. "He is a witness in an investigation. We cannot seize what is already in our custody." The eldest captain chuckled, "you always did underestimate people, Holine. I did warn you this sort of thing might happen." Ilkar began to walk to the exit. "Krell, When you are ready to deliver your testimony, I will have a guard archivist join us in my office. Please don't keep me waiting, I tire quickly these days."

The other captains moved aside, unready to leave, but now reassured that it was not their place to intervene. Krell fixed his gaze on Holine.

Jomran formed a spear of ice and hurled it into the air. Krell dodged it easily, but was in no mood to face his true foe's second in another battle. He swatted a swarm of frozen darts out of the air with a brief wave of heat as he thought of a plan.

"Urun, the Argent Flame, I call on your favor. Come to my aid!" and Krell filled the name with power, spiking a burst of brilliant flame into the ground as he spoke. There was a sound like the tearing of silk, and a smell like melting titanium as Krell's summon opened a path for the Elder Elemental to enter the Imperial Palace. Krell felt the power begin to drain from him as he held the thousand wards at bay to keep Urun within the throne room.

"Krell, I didn't expect to hear you so soon!" the bull-headed burning being buried a fist into one of the ornamental columns and pulled a sword of molten stone from its wreckage. "And you brought me the ones who bound me! Such a thoughtful mage; I like you."

Jomran hesitated as he saw the broad-shouldered elemental, ashen fur rolling down his shoulders. "How? How did you find him? We hid him on..."

"On Gasca? Yes, that is where I found him. The Prince of Elemental Flame bound in a bottle on an enchantress' shelf. I imagine it would take the Frost-bearer himself to overcome his wrath."

Jomran barely summoned his staff in time to block Urun's first blow, and even that was not enough to prevent him from being battered across the room. The junior guards had fully retreated to the steps of the throne, hoping to protect the empress without too much risk to themselves. Krell fed their fear into maintaining Urun's presence as he watched gears turning in Holine's mind. She'd never had her father's mind for lore, but hopefully she'd remembered enough.

Jomran hurled bolt after bolt of ice at the vengeful boar-giant, and although most met their mark, none caused him to so much as falter. He brought up his staff to block another blow, but Urun feinted and kicked him into the steps beneath Holine, before hurling his massive blade into the armored captain. There was no gasp from the captain pinned beneath. As he tried to dislodge the blade, Urun took it in hand, and the massive sword shone like a star as he twisted it free of the dais. Jomran fell limp, and by the time Urun scattered his remains from the end of his blade with a flourish, his armor had grown as soft as butter.

Holine stumbled back up to the throne as Urun turned his wrathful sight on her. She grasped the arm of the throne. A dozen more guards entered the chamber behind Krell as he felt the spell beginning to flicker.

"ZeeGee, the Frost-bearer, Lion That Freezes the Stars. By the power of my throne I summon thee!"

Urun had been called from beyond reality, and so it had been torn to allow the great bull-man entry. Krell smiled as he heard the quiet pop of interstellar teleport. And there, looking up from the foot of the dais from within a mane of ice, was the little otter-lion. After seeing him billow and fill the space of Rea's apartment, it was strange seeing him unable to fill a full step on the stairs that lead to the throne. It was like looking at a cloud in a jar or reading about something you did in a history book; so little space for so much substance.

Small dark eyes peered around the grand room. Its inhabitants now quietly starring at this new visitor. Urun, looked back at Krell, fear rippling through the flaming warrior. "Hey, man, I am really, just super grateful for this opportunity, but I think I should go, like, now." Urun's ember-flecked eyes were focused tightly on the unusually tiny form of the frost elemental.

Krell nodded and released the spell, his own flames quenching as he did. "Thank you for the support, I'll let you know how it goes."

"Destroy the Lich!" Holine commanded. ZeeGee shrank from the sharp command, a single paw raised as he was startled mid-step. He looked at the Empress with confusion and barked back at her. She pointed at Krell, shouting the order once more. He looked at Krell, eyes trembling and then, arching his whole body backward, ZeeGee began to wail despondently. The nearby guards, a thin layer of frost almost imperceptibly creeping up their legs already, shielded their ears from the loud, pathetic cry.

"Really?" Holine, glaring down at ZeeGee's minute form, exclaimed, "this is the Frost-bearer? How were our ancestors so defeated by this pathetic seal that they named a war after him?" She looked up at Krell, but before she could offer further critique, there was a sound like a window shattering, that resonated from every wall and spell.

A woman stood, having appeared no more than five meters from the foot of the dais, and directly between Krell and Holine. Her colorless hair and pale dress was instantly recognizable to even the junior guards, and Krell found the strength to remain standing as he watched Kate's arms rise as she began to gather invisible threads in her hands.

"Give. Him. Back!" there was a tinkling noise as she twisted her hand in the air. A guard, feeling either heroic or desperate charged her from behind, only to be lifted into the air and flung into a nearby column, which shaped itself to bind him like a shackle. This provoked several other guards to begin casting spells; gouts of flame quenched midair, shards of ice evaporated into mist, and missiles of raw energy splashed harmlessly against invisible fields of force, all to no avail. The tinkling began to grow into a high and moving melody as guards began to sink into the floor and be trapped within boxes of transparent force, each unharmed but unable to proceed. The captains, Krell noted, had fully departed the room, choosing to exercise discretion over valor.

"So the great Arcania lives," Holine replied, shouting over ZeeGee's ever-present wail, "it is said that you can no longer take lives, so why should I listen to you?"

"It is true. I accepted an oath to take no further lives." Kate turned both hands now to the unseen strings of magic, playing at that instrument to the sound of falling glass. "But I do not need to take a life to end yours." There was an audible pop as a cloaked man appeared, drawing a knife, and then a crack as a woman with a blaster emerged from a door, which now hung open to somewhere far beyond the palace.

"You've made plenty of enemies. And all they need is an opportunity." A window both mystic and physical crashed as Kate punctuated both song and argument."So give me back my ZeeGee."

The horror on Holine's face, as she watched a half-score assassins emerge from the rapidly collapsing defenses, was only about the seventh most beautiful thing Krell had ever seen, but it was a sight worth remembering. He watched in awe as the handful of remaining guards around the dais began fighting to hold back the ever expanding list of Holine's enemies. Kate stood, unwavering, plucking strings and never taking her eyes off of the Empress.

"Fine! I dismiss you, go back to your mistress, you useless creature!"

Instantly, ZeeGee fell silent, now fully inverted in his slow backward roll, and bounded across the room. He weaved through the skirmish as though it were nothing but rocks in a stream. His body never left a place where his paws hit the ground, but only lengthened and grew as he coiled happily around Kate, who released her magic and pulled him, or at least whatever parts of him she could reach, into a tight embrace.

"You!" Holine called, turning her attention back on Krell, who stood solidly on the ground, still recovering from his own summon. "You're not going anywhere."

She reached out and pulled a familiar locket from some distant part of space, as though it had never been out of her hand. "I may have lost my guard, but at least I can be rid of you too. Say hello to my dad, you meddling bastard!" and she crushed Kevand's necklace in her hand.

Krell felt the Lich shudder, and for a moment he felt relief. The presence that had fought him for control of his own body screamed as it was dragged into the void. Then, he felt his bones start to fall away, collapsing as the magic that held him together unraveled.

Kate looked up, startled, as Krell began to fade. He watched the little otter-lion's expression change, and he finally saw what his ancestors had feared. The room was still, all movement became impossible, and stone cracked as the Frost-bearer bared its jagged teeth. ZeeGee's body swelled until his presence filled the room and his mane was blown wide by an unseen gale as the Lion that Freezes the Stars roared at Holine. He watched her armor crack, and the illusions she'd used to hide her true face vanished as her bones turned to a chill mist. A guard dropped their staff to the ground, dumbfounded, and one of the would-be-assassins, a young man with a forester's pruning hook, cheered as the Empress's hollow shell collapsed and shattered against the Imperial Throne.

As he watched her destruction, Krell thought back. Penalupa's wit and Neleh's devotion had paid off, he'd stopped her. Kevand was avenged, now a true heir could sit on the Imperial Throne. And he'd even managed to keep his end of the bargain with the_Witch. Rea would have her chance to destroy Holine once and for all.

As the last flame of his eyes went out, Krell heard a kind, matronly voice. "Come in soldier. I've baked some cookies and put a kettle on. Lets get you warmed up."

Chapter Sixteen
In Which Cookies Are Offered To All

Rea knew exactly why she had stopped delving through ancient ruins, secret vaults, and hidden temples. The denizens were never the problem. She could do more with a three-inch knife than any five of them could do with blasters. And it wasn't the traps. She was well equipped to avoid those. It was the raw, ostentatious hubris of it all.

Wall after wall depicted Holine's accomplishments: cutting ribbons on warships, commanding soldiers to capture villains, hosting lavish feasts for diplomats. There was no name on a frieze depicting her nobly taking command of a battleship as it fired on a dragon, but Rea remembered Hleaovan and his beloved collection of amethyst geodes she'd stolen from him. As dragons went, he wasn't terribly concerning.

Petra stopped to laugh at a relief showing Holine speaking with the Ga-Vok envoy who had visited the palace five years ago to negotiate an end to a grain tariff. "He looks so bored! Oh, poor Braga, he deserves so much better." Petra touched the stone, and a ripple of energy spread from where her fingers met the relief. The image shifted and the small Ga-Vok male grew and straightened. His expression turned from pleading to patient, even as Holine's image changed from a magnanimous ruler to a looming tyrant, hunching slightly and her casual outstretched hand turned to an accusing single finger.

"There, that should do it justice." She dusted her hand off on her hip and was immediately struck by eighteen poisoned darts from the trap she set off as she leaned onto her back foot to get a better look. Rea reached forward to offer aid before realizing that none had so much as scratched Petra's armor.

"Another one of your students?"

"Of course! I don't know many who weren't at one time or another. This one is fairly recent. The iglakosch is likely close. We should keep going."

The next room was unlocked, and there were no traps within. In the center of the wide, circular chamber was a single figure, chained to the ground by its wrists and ankles. The use of chains was somewhat bizarre, given the dripping slime-like darkness that formed the body of the prisoner. As the two immortals entered the room, Rea reached for her blade. She'd met this foe before, and she wasn't about to meet him unarmed.

"Good Morning my Deadly Darling, you brought a friend today," came a voice from within the mass.

Petra drew her sword and moved in front of Rea, absentmindedly bumping into the witch as she advanced. "Hello Legion. Fancy meeting you here. Did you get yourself trapped again?" She teased, the tip of her blade dragging just enough to make the scratching audible. The paladin began to circle inward toward the imprisoned Shade, and Rea began to skirt the room in the opposite direction, her knife interposed defensively between her and the demon.

"Oh, don't worry Little Witch, I've no intention of letting you curse me again." The lump of slime that sat upon his shoulders was locked upon the knight as it spoke. "I am, I'm afraid, quite devoted to seeing through to fruition the effects of your last curse."

Rea relaxed as little as she could, so as not to alert Petra to her relief. The two had a long-standing rivalry, in no small part caused by Rea's own now ancient spell. Petra, for her part, had no scars from their long history, and Rea knew that she was at greater risk to the demon's wrath, than her friend.

"Rea, go on ahead, I'll catch up after I handle this miscreant." On cue, the Shade slipped his bonds and, with a flourish, the slime flowed down his hand and formed an elegant single-edged blade.

"Another dance? If you insist!" and the Shade charged Petra, and the two began to thrust and parry with the rehearsed precision, in an echo of so many duels past.

Rea darted for the far door, drew a paper charm and slapped it onto the door. The effect was instant, and she fell through the door as though it weren't there, though it stood securely behind her. Whatever chaos came of the duel, she would be unobstructed as she dealt with whatever lay ahead.

The room wasn't terribly large, maybe four meters in diameter. There were three alcoves, forming a perpendicular with the door. The one on the right was empty, but the one on the left contained a partially formed Nieldic skeleton and an Imperial Guard's Bloodstone Staff.

"Who? Intruder!" The skeleton shouted. His arm thrust forward, fingers forming as he fought to reconstitute. Rea ducked his grasp and lunged under his reach to grab the staff. She didn't know who this lackey was, but she knew that a Lich reformed at their iglakosch, and it was the only object in the alcove. He pulled himself forward, staying aloft as his femurs began to weave together. Rea smacked his hands aside with the staff, easy enough with all his strength employed in reforming his body.

"Here goes nothing." Rea swung the long red stave overhead and called out to the spirits of the planet, "Wrath of Medea! Sunder this symbol of your destroyers! Let it be unmade by your might!"

Medea was regarded by most as a dead world, the consequences of a failed early attempt at terraforming. The truth, for she remembered a time when it was still at war with its colonizers, was that the first colonists had plundered the wealth of its nature, and so incurred the wrath of its spirits. It had been a hard lesson for the Nielda, but they had taken it to heart and future efforts had gone more smoothly. The Empire all but abandoned the effort, but those early colonists had not died, and their descendants remained citizens, albeit broken and prone to madness. The spirits had all but died out, but their wrath and fury remained. Now, as Rea called out, she channeled that wrath into the staff, and brought it down upon the bonesteel skull of this final guardian.

The skull dented, but the end of the staff continued to move downward as it cracked in the center. There was a flash of red light and the flames resting in the eyes of the skull diminished, and within moments faded entirely. Rea dropped the fragment she still held, sighed in relief, and turned to inspect the final alcove.

A skull was beginning to form within it. A few glimmers of bonesteel hung beneath it as the spine began to form. But the only thing Rea truly needed was the amulet that hung on a fine ribbon, striped with Imperial blue and purple. There was an image of a chess piece and the words 'Imperial Palace Chess Tourney' on the silver medallion, and an inscription on the back that read 'You'll get me next time kiddo, -Dad'.

"Why is it never a hard metal? It's never 'I have an emotional bond to this marble studded warhammer, or this Diamond shaped like a knife.' Always with the jewelry." Rea looked at the skull as the jaw began to grow more defined. Two flames flicked into existence and the skull began to stir. Rea reached up and took the medal out of the alcove.

Holine's still forming body tumbled helplessly to the ground, her strength apparently spent.

"What are you doing here? Did Krell send a child to finish me off?"

"Well, aren't we presuming a lot about the situation."

The skull laughed, ribs beginning to grow from the spine. "So you do know the old fool. Well you can just give up then, he's already dead."

Rea paused. It was a risk. They'd all known it could happen. "He's a lich, he'll be back soon enough."

"I crushed his iglakosch, he's not coming back from that." Her shoulder blades were beginning to form, and the skeletal torso began to hover slightly off the ground. "So you people's hope of rebellion can rot. I am Empress, and I will not be removed!"

Rea took a step back. She was afraid for a moment, and then she felt the weight in her hand. She hung her head, feeling the weight of the medallion. She let the weight of the words flow down her like pudding, slowly and unpleasantly.

"I would have gotten away with it too if it weren't for that stupid, misshapen elemental and Arcania. But once I get back to the palace, I'm going to hunt them down," A single hand clacked against the stone walls, "And I'm going to do what my ancestors lacked the strength to do. What they should have done!"

Rea activated the golden bangles hanging at her wrists, feeling their leaden weight added to that of the medallion, and she brought it over her head and swung the enchanted metal disk into the skeletal wrist of the fallen Empress. It split the magical bonds, and she could feel the thin lines of power fall loose from the iglakosch she wielded.

"What you should have done is left people alone!" Rea yelled as she wound up for another strike. The Lich recoiled, hand-less and in pain for the first time in a lifetime. The next blow struck her knee, flattening the side of the medallion as the force of the blow scattered the no longer enchanted limb.

"He would have lived, what, forty years? Fifty?!" Rea's next swing went wide as Holine withdrew, jaw wide in shock. "Instead you made a good man into a weapon." Stone shattered as the amulet impacted against it, the protective enchantments keeping it from being broken by a missed blow. "You stole his only death! For what? Spite?!" Rea's next blow cracked the medallion as Holine blocked with what remained of her right arm. "You selfish! Ignorant! Brat!" Each blow was punctuated by a rib cracking strike, and the medallion's condition continued to worsen as Rea beat the Lich back into her alcove.

Holine no longer hovered. Her one remaining arm was held aloft, shielding her from further blows, and even with naught but flame and bone her fear was obvious. Rea hesitated, thinking of the inscription on the medallion she held, of a father's love.

And then she pictured the robed man she'd watched plead with an Imperial Guard not to fight, and she thought of a man, passing his infant daughter to his best friend, and telling him that he knew she'd be safe with him.

"You should have let him live, because if you had, I wouldn't be standing over you now." Rea battered away the arm, and stared deeply into the flames. She felt the seconds ticking, but she didn't need a clock to know the hour of Holine's death, the time was right. She brought the battered piece of silver down in a wide, arcing strike that knocked the jaw loose and broke the medal. There was no sound, no rippling enchantment, only stillness in the Hearth of Holine IV. Rea dropped the broken trophy, turned to the door, and walked away.

A door opened, and a stout, matronly woman with wings that blocked the hall behind her and eyes that seemed to blink out from every part of her stood in the doorway. Rea could smell berry tea, lemon-scented floor polish, and fresh cookies within the chamber beyond.

"Hello dear. It's been a while, but I have something for you."

Rea was silent in the presence of Death Herself. She'd killed too many, for far too long, to not be familiar with the voice and face of the last guide. But it had been some thousands of years since they had fought beside each other, and only one of them had returned from the Demonwastes of Anatolia.

"It's alright. I'd be surprised too if I knew what you knew." She turned back into the kitchen and shouted, "Please take a few for Rea too. She can't come in and get any and I can't take any out to her. Use the tin on top of the pantry." Then, turning back to Rea, "I know how much you always enjoyed my baking, and it's so rare I get to send anyone back I just had to make extra for you."

"How is this happening? We watched you die!"

"That's not saying much dear. You've watched a lot of people die." She smiled, and brushed some flour off of her long plain black dress, only managing to knock the flour off into one of her many eyelashes. "What's much more special, and you especially can appreciate this, is that today, you get to watch somebody live." Death turned around and beckoned forward a confused looking young man holding a small tin, covered in images of needles and thread, which smelled of chocolate and butter.

"Young man, be sure to share those with your friends. Now go on back outside, and remember to use your feet. The last fellow tripped almost at once, and I would hate to see you scuff your nice new body so quickly." And she gently pushed him through the door, waving gently. "Take care of my daughter Rea. She has some big days coming up, and she's going to need an honest heart beside her."

Before Rea could respond, the door closed as though blown shut by an unseen wind. As the elder woman vanished, a thousand eyes winking as the image faded into reality, a black sword pushed effortlessly through the door and cut open the locks Rea had avoided. The door slid open, revealing Petra, sweaty and smiling.

"Who's this? You should have mentioned we had a fourth."

The young man adjusted the tin of cookies into his off-hand and offered the other to the knight in only slightly less than shining armor. "You must be Petra. Name's Krell Casat. I'm a friend of Rea's"

Iglakosch – an object used to tether a soul to the world, preventing them from returning from death

Krell - Krel – A main character, a lich and of late an admiral

Rea – rAy-uh – A main character, the_Witch and an immortal

Nielda – Nee-El-duh – A race that, although appearing human are very much not, also used in reference to the primary nation within which the events of this book unfold.

Gasca – Gas-kuh – A temperate, earth-like planet with a long history, part of the Nieldic Empire

Ga-Vok – guh-vOk – A race of short, canid humanoids with which the Nielda have a long history

Seclora – Seh-Klor-uh – A rival nation to the Nieldic empire, and predominantly comprised of Nielda

Holine – Ho-lean – a villain, and the current Empress of the Nieldic Empire

Atalaine – Ah-tuh-lAne – An Enchanter and member of the Gascan royal family

Alicea – Al-ih-See-uh – The progenitor of the Gascan royal family, and a friend of Rea's

Medea – meh-Dee-uh – A barren, earth-like planet, and part of the Nieldic Empire

Athalion – Að-al-E-on – Current king of Gasca, father of Atalaine

Urun – oo-Roon – A fire Elemental, looking one half man, one half boar.

ZeeGee – (please don't make me explain this one) – A frost Elemental and familiar to kate, looks like
an otter-lion

Gravaga – Gruh-Vah-guh – A nation of crystalline servants and warriors loyal to their creator, the Dark Lady.

Don't miss out!

Visit the website below and you can sign up to receive emails whenever D. E. Stone publishes a new book. There's no charge and no obligation.

https://books2read.com/r/B-A-OUOH-NYQTB

BOOKS2READ

Connecting independent readers to independent writers.

About the Author

Since early childhood Daniel always preferred to spend his time absorbed in fantastical worlds like The Lord Of The Rings and Star Wars. Deciding that they simply weren't enough he added as many worlds as he could to his mindscape including real world myths. This resulted in a world of his own: rich with science fiction, comic-esque heroes and villains, high fantasy, and gads of sass. He honed his craft publishing his works on a blog in 2009. He now spends his time building stories with his horde of feisty princesses (his wife and daughters) in the Middle of the West, United States.

Read more at https://motleymince.com/.